Nobody said no to body language like that

Tyler also knew that nobody said no to a woman who looked and smelled, sounded and felt like Jenna.

He needed to stop this. He needed to let her down easy. She was the subject of his investigation, for goodness sakes.

"Tyler?" she breathed. She closed her eyes and leaned into him.

He clenched his hands into fists, trying to get the right words, the right phrases to form in his mind. But they didn't. There was no way out of this without kissing her. Just a taste, he promised himself.

Aw, hell. Tyler gently pressed his lips against hers, but promised he wouldn't pucker.

Jenna wound her arms around him, her soft body cradling his tightly.

A roar started in his ears and quickly overwhelmed his brain. Forget puckering, his lips parted. She tasted of sweet wine and summer sunshine.

Damn.

Dear Reader,

I love a hero with a secret. I particularly love a hero who has to choose between his secret and his principles. Add to that a sexy heroine who tempts him to compromise both, and you've got Tyler Reeves, private investigator, a man going quietly insane while he watches the one woman in the world he can't possibly touch.

Growing up in Vancouver, Canada, I often drove with my family across the border to visit Seattle. With its towering hotels, exciting shopping and extraordinarily beautiful scenery, it remains one of my favorite cities. The last time I visited, my good friend Jane Porter drove me along the winding lakeshore roads to view the magnificent homes set between cedar forests and the rocky shore. This laid-back luxury was the inspiration for the Quayside hotel, the fictional setting for *Next to Nothing!*

I had a great time writing this story. I hope you enjoy the atmosphere of the West Coast.

Best wishes,

Barbara Dunlop

Books by Barbara Dunlop

HARLEQUIN TEMPTATION
848—FOREVER JAKE

HARLEQUIN DUETS
54B—THE MOUNTIE STEALS A WIFE

Don't miss any of our special offers. Write to us at the following address for information on our newest releases.

Harlequin Reader Service
U.S.: 3010 Walden Ave., P.O. Box 1325, Buffalo, NY 14269
Canadian: P.O. Box 609, Fort Erie, Ont. L2A 5X3

Next to Nothing!
Barbara Dunlop

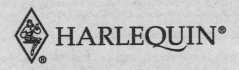

HARLEQUIN®

TORONTO • NEW YORK • LONDON
AMSTERDAM • PARIS • SYDNEY • HAMBURG
STOCKHOLM • ATHENS • TOKYO • MILAN • MADRID
PRAGUE • WARSAW • BUDAPEST • AUCKLAND

For my editor, Kathryn Lye.
Thank you for your advice and encouragement,
and most of all for your unfailing patience.

ISBN 0-373-69101-7

NEXT TO NOTHING!

Copyright © 2002 by Barbara Dunlop.

Visit us at www.eHarlequin.com

Printed in U.S.A.

"HE STILL OUT THERE?" Jenna McBride watched as her business partner, Candice Hammond, crossed in front of the waterfall fountain in the hospital's new atrium lobby.

"Short guy?" asked Candice, her high heels clicking on the freshly finished sienna tile floor. "Balding. Doesn't know polyester is dead?" She spoke loudly enough to be heard above the rushing water.

"That's him." Jenna snapped her pencil into the clasp at the top of her Canna Interiors clipboard. The closed-for-construction lobby was nearly empty now that most of the workers had left for the day. "Where on earth did Brandon find that guy?"

Jenna's partner in Canna Interiors arched her perfect eyebrows, her dark lips curving up in a half smile that revealed the dimple in her left cheek. "One-nine-hundred aging gumshoe?"

Jenna shook her head and raked her auburn, shoulder-length hair back from her forehead. She was hot from working all day, and a fine sheen of sweat dampened her hairline.

"I can't believe he's still trying." She'd finally broken off her engagement to Brandon four months ago. Then she'd moved from Boston to Seattle to put some distance between them.

"You always did live in denial," said Candice as she settled on the bench facing the fountain, crossing one stocking-clad leg over the other. "Ol' Brandon's like the Energizer Bunny."

"Not in bed," scoffed Jenna, surprising herself with the moment of pithy honesty.

Candice's eyes lit up with newfound admiration and humor. She sat slightly forward. "You've come a long way, baby."

"Because I no longer think the sun rises and sets on Brandon Rice?" Jenna took a seat at the opposite end of the bench, curling one denim-covered calf beneath the opposite leg and setting her clipboard down next to her purse.

It was embarrassing to realize she'd been taken in so easily, and for such a long time. Naive and gullible. Book smart and life stupid. That was Jenna.

"Because you can finally admit he was a loser in bed," said Candice, gazing at the water as it foamed against the natural rocks and sculpted mortar. Her short, chic hair curled against the collar of her jacket.

"It was kind of hard to tell in the thick of things," said Jenna. She eased off her loafers, wiggling her toes.

The high ceiling fans sent a light breeze wafting

down, but the mid-June sunshine had warmed the atrium.

Candice fought a smirk.

"It's not like I'd done any comparison shopping," Jenna added. "I was barely twenty-two when we met."

She was twenty-six now. And, thanks to Candice, she had a second chance on life. A chance that didn't include becoming Mrs. Brandon Rice—properly behaved trophy wife. Or was that properly behaved lap dog? Hard to know for sure.

"You don't need vast personal experience to know three minutes is pathetic," said Candice, giving her head a shake and rattling her silver earrings. "You just need the public library." She cocked her head, contemplating the newly finished fountain. "You think the whale is too much?"

"The whale is perfect," said Jenna, turning her attention to the brightly painted stone sculpture spouting beneath the waterfall, which was surrounded by tropical plants.

Forget uptight, three-minute Brandon, the kids were going to love that whale. The hospital board had asked for something with child-appeal when they'd given Canna Interiors the contract to decorate the pediatric lobby. Other than that, Candice and Jenna had been given a pretty free hand in the conceptual designs.

Jenna was proud of the results.

A collection of jumbo African animals adorned one corner. They were made of durable acrylic, and perfectly suited to climbing. Comfortable furniture groupings and lush plants dotted the high, glass-ceilinged room, and the carpet was a maze of brightly colored pathways twisting among cute, brown monkeys.

A week, maybe two at the most, and it would be ready to open. They were on time and on budget. And, on the strength of this project's success, they'd been invited to submit designs to the public library.

A design invitation wasn't a guarantee, but Jenna was finally beginning to feel optimistic about the future. After Candice had helped her see Brandon for the control freak he was, they'd moved clear across the country and pumped their life savings into a new interior design firm.

Though Jenna's financial contribution was much lower than her friend's, Candice had insisted they become equal partners. Jenna was determined to work day and night to prove her friend's faith was justified.

"Why don't you call him?" asked Candice, turning to peer enigmatically at Jenna.

"Call Brandon?" Jenna tucked her loose hair behind her ear, fingering the small gold stud in her lobe.

She hadn't spoken to her ex-fiancé since she'd left him. In fact, it was Candice who'd insisted she break all ties. They'd burned all his letters, kept their apartment phone number unlisted and screened calls at the office.

"You want me to call Brandon?" Jenna repeated, having trouble with her friend's about-face.

"Yes. I do." Candice sat up straighter. "Maybe I was wrong."

"You? Wrong?"

"I know." Candice waved a hand in the air. "It's hard to believe. But, maybe you should tell him once and for all that it's over."

"I told him it was over when I left," said Jenna, reaching for the pencil in her clipboard, releasing it from the spring and tapping the eraser against the top page. She really had no desire to speak to Brandon again.

"You were upset then, hurt, confused. He probably thought you'd calm down and come to your senses."

"I did come to my senses. That's why I left him."

"Apparently Brandon needs a bit more convincing."

Jenna palmed the pencil and stood up. "You know, the minute I call him, he's going to try to talk me into coming back."

Candice folded her manicured fingers together on her knee, tipping her chin in Jenna's direction. "Would you?" she asked calmly.

"*No!* Definitely not." Not a chance in a million. Jenna absolutely did not want to live the rest of her life in a gilded cage, letting Brandon choose her clothes, her jewelry, her hair color. She'd had a taste of freedom, and she loved it.

"Well, as long as you keep hiding from him—"

"I am *not* hiding. You're the one who—"

"He'll convince himself you still have feelings for him," Candice finished.

"There are no feelings. Period." As she spoke the words, Jenna realized just how true they were. There was nothing. No hatred, no anger, no fear.

Flat line.

She hadn't been intimidated by him, maybe over-awed. Brandon had been a strong-minded, confident, charismatic guest lecturer at Boston University. While Jenna had been an impressionable undergraduate, fresh from a Minnesota farm community. It was pretty easy for him to convince her that he knew best—in all things.

But those feelings were gone now. Jenna took a deep breath, inhaling the light fountain mist and the scent of the pepper trees. She was free.

Sure she'd call Brandon. There was no reason not to anymore.

"Think about it, Jenna." Candice interrupted her thoughts. "Call him and let him know that malleable young woman doesn't exist anymore. Then he'll back off and call off his troops."

"You're right," said Jenna with conviction. Candice always did give the best advice.

"I am?" Candice looked surprised by Jenna's easy agreement.

"You bet. He needs to know it's over. He needs to leave me alone. We can't have rent-a-Dick-Tracy hanging around the hospital halls scaring the children."

Candice grinned as she stood up and flipped a concealed switch to turn off the waterfall. "Go get 'im, Jenna." The whirring motor stopped, and the water dripped to a halt against the huge lava rocks, plunking to silence in the cavernous room.

Jenna nodded decisively, retrieving her tiny cell phone from the depths of her big purse. It was a serious purse, not one of those elegant little evening bags that Brandon bought her. They barely held a comb.

Using the end of the pencil, she dialed quickly.

Hopefully, someday soon, she'd forget his private number and free up the brain space for something useful. She lifted the phone to her ear, and Candice gave her an encouraging grin.

Brandon picked up on the first ring.

Little wonder. The only people who knew this number were his mother, a few captains of industry, some dubious politicians and Jenna.

"Rice here," he said in that unnaturally low tone that he thought made him sound three inches taller.

"It's Jenna," she said, voice crisp and impersonal.

"Jenna!" His voice brightened and rose an octave.

"Finally. Where are you sweetheart?" He sounded so happy, so satisfied, so smug.

"You know darn well where I am. Your hired goon is standing outside my job-site."

Candice gave her a thumbs-up.

"Goon? What goon? You're talking nonsense." His low voice was back. He was displeased. Good.

He was on the other side of the country. He could be as displeased as he wanted, and it wouldn't affect her.

"Call him off, Brandon."

"Jenna," he sighed, and his tone turned patronizing. "Let's not start this out by arguing."

"I'm not arguing. I'm stating a fact."

"You need to calm down and listen, Jenny-Penny."

"Don't call me that."

"I don't know what Candice told you—"

"This isn't about what Candice did or did not tell me."

"I always knew she was a bad influence."

Jenna's voice rose, and she paced in a little half circle on the cool floor. "Give me some credit, Brandon. I can make up my own mind. I can make my own choices—"

"Is it about the surgery?"

"Yes!" She spun back to face Candice. The plastic surgery, and so much more.

"It's already cancelled."

"You bet your life it's cancelled. So are my hair appointments and my spa membership. You might want me to have a perfect nose and sculpted abs, but that doesn't mean I—"

Candice's eyes went wide. She made a frantic *calm down* motion with her hand.

Jenna paused for a breath, raking her hand once more through her hair. Her auburn hair—a little bright, a little gaudy, but her own natural color.

"Jenna, honey, you just had to say so."

Yeah. Right. Jenna scoffed silently and shook her head. Like her opinion about her body or anything else had ever counted.

"Brandon," she began again, calmer this time. Resolute. "I am not the right person for you. And you are not the right person for me. Can we please leave it at that?"

Candice nodded, admiration in her eyes.

"So, that's it?" asked Brandon, voice hardening. "You finally call and it's to break up?"

"We broke up four months ago."

"You had a tantrum four months ago."

Jenna clenched her jaw. She would not rise to the bait. She was calm, in control. "Call it whatever you like. We're through."

"So, you think that's it? You expect me to tell my colleagues that my little fiancée up and left me? Pawn the ring? Eat the ballroom deposit?"

"You can tell your colleagues any damn thing you want." Jenna pressed two fingers tight against her forehead. She wondered how he'd explained her absence for the past four months. But she sure wasn't going to ask him.

Brandon snorted derisively into the phone. He hated it when she swore. It wasn't ladylike.

"And call off the damn P.I.," she added for good measure.

The phone cracked as Brandon hung up, and she jerked it away from her ear.

Candice flinched, and they stared at each other in silence for a moment.

"Shall we take that as a yes?" asked Candice.

"I'm assuming so." A sheepish grin pulled up the corners of Jenna's mouth. Gosh, that had felt good.

"SAY IT ISN'T SO." Tyler Reeve's older brother Derek filled the doorway of his office. Derek's chin was tipped up, and his arms were folded across his broad chest.

Tyler swore under his breath, following Derek's gaze to the duffel and the damning sleeping bag, which he'd carelessly dropped on the couch an hour ago. "It isn't so," he deadpanned, turning his attention back to his computer monitor.

"Striker said things were bad, but jeez..." Derek took a step into Tyler's outer office and kicked the door shut behind him.

"Striker should mind his own business," said Tyler, referring to the middle Reeves brother. He punched in the password to his personal bank account on the receptionist's computer, hoping to see that the lawyer's escrow deposit had added a few zeros to his balance.

"At least come out and stay in the guest house," said Derek.

"No thanks."

"This is stubborn even for you."

"I got myself into this mess. I'll get myself out." The deposit hadn't cleared. Tyler closed his eyes for a second.

He needed that money. Needed it today. He'd already cleaned out his savings account.

He'd taken a chance in writing Mrs. Cliff a check last night for her car, but it was either that or admit to the whole world that the IPS Detective Agency was broke—admit to the world that he'd been stupid enough to trust a partner who'd defrauded the company along with several of their clients.

Tyler would just as soon get shot.

Again.

In a place far more painful than his shoulder.

"Why does 'getting yourself out of this mess' have to involve eating cheap takeout food and sleeping on a short couch?" Derek crossed the room and picked up the corner of Tyler's old Boy Scout sleeping bag.

"Because I sold the beach house." Giving up on the bank balance for now, Tyler pushed back the chair and stood up. He preferred to look Derek in the eye for this conversation.

Derek might be six foot two, but Tyler had caught up to him on his eighteenth birthday, and even managed to beat him by half an inch. Not that it mattered. He was now and always would be the little brother.

And linebacker Derek could still take him out without even breaking a sweat.

"Because you were too stubborn to ask the family for help," corrected Derek.

"A thirty-year-old man does not go running to his daddy for help just because his business hits a little snag."

"A little *snag?*" Derek's voice was incredulous.

"A little snag," Tyler echoed.

"Your partner skipped with your clients' money."

Tyler gritted his teeth. "I'm handling it."

"I can accept that you didn't want to go to Dad. But why didn't you come to me or Striker?"

Tyler folded his arms across his chest, imitating his brother's pose. "I needed money, Derek. And I needed it fast."

It had been forty-eight hours since he discovered Reggie's duplicity, but saying it out loud still stung. Tyler had to squelch an urge to bash his fist into the nearest wall. It was an urge he'd been battling for two days.

"How much did you sell it for?" asked Derrick.

Tyler named a sum that made Derrick's eyes widen.

"That's it? You practically *gave* the beach house away."

"They offered cash."

"*I* would've bought it for that."

"And I'd still have a place to live?"

"Exactly."

"I'm not a charity case."

Derek's booming voice rose. "Jeez, Tyler, lightning won't strike you dead if you borrow a little family money."

"You know as well as I do that once Dad gets his hooks in me, I'll be his for life."

"Like me, you mean."

"No. Not like you. You genuinely want to stare at balance sheets and stock portfolios all day long. Though how you've managed to stay sane this long is beyond me."

Derek was the golden boy, the heir apparent to Reeves-DuCarter International, the pride and joy of three generations. Meanwhile, Tyler was the black sheep.

Derek shook his head. "You never did understand—"

"I understand perfectly. I'm thirty years old. This private eye thing isn't just a phase. It's my vocation, my dream, my calling."

"Doin' real well for you so far" Derek snorted.

Tyler winced. "It's a small setback."

"How much did he get?"

"Reggie?"

"No." Derek rolled his eyes. "Of course Reggie."

Tyler slumped back down in the chair. "What did Striker tell you?"

Derek pulled up a guest chair and folded his big body into it. "That Reggie split with a client's car and a cashier's check."

Tyler nodded. That about summed it up. Reggie had also made free with several hundred thousand in retainers over the past few months, much of which Tyler would have to pay back since Reggie wasn't around to do the work.

"How much?" Derek repeated.

"Including Mrs. Cliff's BMW?"

"Quit stalling."

Tyler voiced the amount that still made him wince. "But I suspect most of it went up his nose before the big disappearing act."

The books were a mess.

Tyler's life was a mess.

Derek let out a long, slow whistle. "What's plan B?"

Tyler gave a chopped, terse chuckle. Plan A implicitly being to hunt Reggie down and take it out of his hide. "Pay Mrs. Cliff for the car—I told her we wrecked it—back out of Reggie's contracts and eat the penalties, sleep in the office for a while, find some quick, high-paying jobs..."

Derek glanced around the reception area with a frown.

"I've got coffee, a bath, a deli on the first floor," said Tyler. "What more does a man need?"

"Bunk out at my place," said Derek.

Tyler shook his head. "I don't want Dad to know what's going on."

Derek stared hard into Tyler's eyes, but Tyler didn't flinch.

Derek was a fixer, just like their father. Tyler knew it was nearly killing him to sit back and watch his little brother stumble.

But Tyler was not giving in. He'd learned years ago that if he didn't fight tooth and nail for every little scrap of independence, he'd end up in a Saville Row suit in a cushy office on the top floor of the Reeves-DuCarter building in downtown Seattle chatting nonsense with overseas investors and monitoring the Dow Jones Industrial Average.

"This isn't high school, Derek. Let me handle it this time."

Derek drew back in his chair. "One guy. I punched out *one guy* for you."

Tyler shook his head. "Blackburn and his friends harassed me for three years thanks to you." Finally, in Tyler's senior year, he'd grown big enough to flatten Blackburn on his own and put a stop to the relentless tormenting.

"*What?*" Derek rocked forward. His fists balled. "They kept at it? Why didn't you tell me?"

Tyler threw up his hands. "So you could punch him out again? Please, Derek. There's nothing more pathetic than a kid who can't fight his own battles."

"Blackburn was twice your size."

Tyler cracked a half smile. "Not in the end, he wasn't."

Derek's eyes flashed with sudden admiration. "*You* were the one who broke his nose?"

"I was the one who broke his nose. I solved that problem. And I'll solve this one, too. It just might take me a while."

Derek glanced around the office again. "Well, there's no need to be a martyr about it. Why not take a suite at the Quayside?"

"Because I'm trying to save money."

"You're a shareholder. They'll give you a rate."

"Rate's zero if I stay here."

The phone on the desktop rang.

"Where's Shirley?" asked Derek.

"Had to cut her back to part-time."

"*What?* You can't even afford one employee?"

The phone rang again.

"Cash flow," said Tyler. "It's just temporary. She wanted to spend some time with her kids for the summer anyway." He picked up the receiver. "IPS Detectives."

Derek gazed at the ceiling and shook his head, as if invoking divine intervention.

"Reggie Sandhill," said a man's curt voice.

"Reggie is out of the country for a few weeks," said Tyler.

Derek snorted at Tyler's lie.

Tyler ignored him. "I'm his partner, Tyler Reeves."

"Reggie came highly recommended," said the man, in a tone that told Tyler he wasn't used to disappointment.

"Perhaps I can help you." said Tyler evenly, annoyed by both the man's attitude and by Reggie's habit of taking all the glory for cases that Tyler had solved. Everyone knew Reggie's name. Nobody knew Tyler's.

"It's a surveillance job," said the man on the phone, a challenge in his voice.

Like, maybe Tyler couldn't handle surveillance. "No problem. Surveillance is one of our specialties."

"I see." The man seemed to be weighing whether or not to trust Tyler. "Her name is Jenna McBride," he finally said.

"And your name?" asked Tyler, picking up a pencil and pulling a scratch pad closer on the desktop.

There was a slight hesitation on the line. "Brandon Rice. She's my fiancée."

"You think she's cheating?" asked Tyler. Cheating

was far and away the most common reason for a man to have his significant other followed.

Derek stood up, pacing across the room, a scowl on his face. Chasing cheating fiancées was obviously not his idea of a stellar career move. Too bad. It wasn't like Tyler was in a position to be choosy. True, it wasn't his usual area of business, but this was the kind of job he needed right now—quick, uncompli- cated cash.

"Yes," said Brandon Rice. "I think she's cheating. I'm in Boston, and she's in Seattle. I want a full report on her activities. Where she goes, who she sees. She has a decorating business. Canna Interiors."

Tyler jotted down the woman's name and the name of her business. "Is there anyone in particular you think she's seeing?"

Derek made a disgusted sound in the back of his throat and shook his head. Well, hell, every case couldn't be a crown jewel theft or a murder mystery. A guy still had to pay the bills.

Some days more than others.

"I want to know everything," said Brandon. "Money is not an issue. I want to know *everyone* she sees. *Everything* she does."

Tyler tapped the pencil eraser against the desktop. Reggie had taken on cases like this before. Rich man, pretty woman, edge of desperation. There was prob- ably a big age difference.

"I'll pay you ten thousand plus expenses," said Brandon. "One week. A full report. And I mean *full*."

Tyler resisted the urge to scowl at the phone, aware of Derek's keen interest. He always submitted a full report to his clients—no matter what his opinion of them.

If this fiancée had any brains at all, she'd stay in Seattle and well away from Mr. Demanding. Of course, she was the one who'd agreed to marry the guy in the first place.

She was probably willing to put up with his crap for the money. Women generally did forgive a whole lot of ills for a whole lot of bank balance.

"When do you want me to start?" asked Tyler.

"Today," barked Brandon. "I want you to start today."

"You got it," said Tyler. "Where do I send the report?"

After jotting down Brandon's contact information, Tyler hung up the phone.

"You're going to follow a cheating wife?" asked Derek.

"Fiancée," Tyler corrected, feeling a twinge of self-consciousness.

"But you won't lower yourself to join the family firm and negotiate with offshore investors?"

"You really want to help me?" asked Tyler, ignoring his big brother's sarcasm, pretending it didn't bite. From experience Tyler knew the best way to get Derek off his back was to give him a mission.

"Name it," said Derek, pulling his checkbook out of his suit pocket.

"I'm not taking your money. If you really want to be useful, you can head over to Canna Interiors."

Without Reggie as a second body, Tyler was handicapped. "I need to know how many employees are there. What kind of an outfit it is. And what Jenna McBride looks like. But I can't let her see me yet."

"Can I have one of those fountain pen cameras and a decoder ring?" asked Derek.

"Don't be an ass." Tyler stood up and shoved his big brother toward the door.

"But, Tyler, how am I going to *case the joint* without the proper James Bond paraphernalia?"

"Just tell me what she looks like, and what they do, so I can make a plan." That ten thousand would go a long way towards operating expenses for the next couple of months.

2

"JENNA MCBRIDE?"

Jenna stopped short, halfway into the Canna Interiors offices as the large man rose from a white leather chair in the reception area.

"Mr. Reeves has been waiting for half an hour," said her secretary, Rosemary, a lilt of excitement in her voice, and an appreciative glimmer in her eyes.

Rosemary was a grandmother in her early fifties, but Jenna could see why a woman of any age might find the burly Mr. Reeves attractive. She heard Candice suck in a quick, admiring breath behind her.

"Yes. I'm Jenna McBride." She moved toward the waiting area, hand extended. "And this is my partner Candice Hammond." For an impish moment, Jenna considered adding the fact that Candice was single.

"Derek Reeves," said the man, grasping Jenna's hand.

Then he turned to Candice and gave her a cursory glance and a nod.

"Candice," said Candice, offering her hand.

He shook it with an absent nod, then he immediately turned back to Jenna. "I was wondering if we might talk for a few minutes?"

She felt Candice stiffen.

Jenna half turned her head to smile in Candice's direction in an effort to include her. "How can *we* help you?"

Derek Reeves gestured to the low table in the reception area. "I've been reviewing your portfolio." He still spoke directly to Jenna. He almost seemed to be studying her face.

"You're interested in the services of a decorating firm?" she asked politely. Judging by the cut of his suit, Derek could be a great prospective customer.

"Uh...yeah." He nodded. "That's right. I am."

"We'll probably be more comfortable in the boardroom." Jenna gestured to an open doorway behind the receptionist's desk. While the man's attention switched to the boardroom door, she signaled to the coffeepot.

Rosemary gave her a quick nod of understanding.

Derek Reeves glanced at Candice, then back at Jenna. He cleared his throat. "Sounds fine."

"I have a conference call in about two minutes," Candice quickly inserted, obviously picking up the same strange signals as Jenna. "Do you mind, Jenna?"

"Of course not." Jenna reminded herself that Derek was the customer, and Candice was acting like a professional. Still, she couldn't help feeling a little annoyed on Candice's behalf. "I'll bring you up to speed later."

"Great. Thanks." Candice turned a stiff smile on Derek. "Nice to meet you Mr. Reeves."

"Likewise," he replied formally, again with barely a glance.

Ignoring the obvious undercurrent, Jenna led Derek Reeves into the small boardroom.

"Why don't you tell me a little bit about your project," she suggested as they sat down at the polished, round table. The deep patina absorbed the late day sun. Candice had insisted their offices exude success, even before they had their first client. Jenna found herself glad of that right now.

"Sure." Derek paused, glancing around at the sample pictures on the wall of the room. "Good idea... It's a...lobby." He stopped scanning the walls and sat back. "A lobby."

"Oh." Jenna waited a moment for him to elaborate. "Would that be in an office building?"

His forehead furrowed and he glanced around the room again. "Yes. I mean, no. It's a...hotel." He slowly smiled and nodded as if he'd just had a mental revelation. "A *hotel* lobby."

Jenna experienced a twinge of disappointment. So far, they didn't have any experience decorating hotels. They'd started with private homes and branched out to some office buildings. The hospital lobby was their big break into special purpose space, but she didn't think whale fountains and monkey carpets would impress many hotel owners.

Her uncertainty must have shown, because Derek jumped back in.

"Did I say lobby?" he asked.

"Yes..."

"Well, actually, it's more than just the lobby." He nodded. "It's the restaurant, too."

"The restaurant?" Her heart sank. They had absolutely nothing in the way of experience that would qualify them to decorate a restaurant.

"And," Derek continued, "well, the spa, too. In fact, you know, the whole hotel should really be upgraded."

"The *whole* hotel?" Jenna's eyes widened.

"Right."

"Uh, Mr. Reeves—"

"Call me Derek."

"Sure. Derek." Jenna debated the merits of blunt honesty versus the incredible opportunity of decorating an entire hotel. She wanted the job. She wanted the job very, very much. But there was the touchy matter of experience.

"It sounds like..." she tried. "I mean, of course we'd be delighted to submit..." A little voice inside her told her to shut up and say yes. "Uh, is the hotel here in Seattle?"

"Yes. On the lake. The Quayside."

"The *Quayside?*" Jenna's heart stopped for a split second. She felt the blood drain from her face.

"You've heard of it?"

"Yes. Of course." Who *hadn't* heard of the Quayside? Jenna dropped her hands into her lap and pinched herself.

The Quayside was a gorgeous, venerated historic hotel on a scenic point of land right on the shore of Lake Washington. It was an architectural dream, water on three sides, and a stunning view of the Cascade Mountain range.

It had played host to business magnates, movie stars and royalty. This was a job which could catapult their firm to the stratosphere.

Jenna swallowed. *Do not mess this up.* "We could draft some preliminary sketches—"

"Tell you what." Derek rose from the table, and Jenna followed suit. "I'll give you my card." He reached into his suit jacket pocket. Then he flipped the card over and pulled out a pen.

"I'm writing the name and phone number of the hotel manager on the back. Give me a few... Uh, I mean, give *him* a call. But wait until late tomorrow afternoon. He'll give you the details."

Jenna nodded silently. Her brain was running a million miles an hour. Candice was going to die. She was going to fall off her chair and die right there in the office.

Derek straightened up and handed Jenna the card. "Thank you, Mr.... Derek."

He smiled, and his eyes lit up like Santa Claus. "Thank *you*, Jenna."

TYLER SNAPPED a couple of pictures from the Quayside Hotel parking lot as Jenna and her partner Candice emerged from the front entry. Derek had called last night to describe Jenna, and to tell Tyler she currently had a contract at the hospital. From there, Tyler had followed the pair to the hotel.

Jenna seemed to be having the time of her life with her fiancé out of the picture. The two women walked down the sidewalk, talking animatedly, laughing, and gesturing in the air like a couple of college students as they headed for Candice's sedan.

Tyler raised his newspaper so that it shielded his face as they passed his SUV. Whatever had happened in the hotel, they were certainly excited about it. He wondered for a moment if they'd met their boyfriends. It was a definite possibility.

As their vehicle backed out of the space, he turned his attention to the stone building, training the camera in preparation for the emergence of their dates. He could catch up with the women at either the hospital or the Canna Interiors office later.

A family emerged from the hotel, then a lone businessman, then...nobody. Five minutes went by, then ten, then fifteen. Finally, the door opened again. But it was an elderly couple who stopped to talk to the doorman.

Okay, so Jenna and Candice weren't meeting men for a clandestine lunchtime date. At least not men who were leaving the hotel a discreet few minutes after them.

He supposed they could have met men who were

guests at the hotel, who didn't need to come out to the parking lot after lunch. But that was stretching his initial theory a little too far.

He placed the camera on the seat beside him and reached for the ignition key. He could go inside and talk to Henry Wenchel, the hotel manager. Henry was an old friend of the family and, technically at least, Tyler was still a company shareholder. But the odds of Henry having noticed two women having lunch in one of the restaurants were ridiculously small.

Except that they were unusually attractive. Candice was tall and willowy, with a fresh, wind-blown supermodel look that would turn any head. Jenna was shorter, a bit more understated. But her thick, auburn hair was gorgeous, and there was something about her smile and the glint in her sea-foam eyes that made Tyler think it was a shame she was being wasted on Brandon Rice.

None of his business, he reminded himself. Rich men and gorgeous women had been making marriage deals since time immemorial. His job was to see if she was making side deals with anyone else.

He pulled out of the parking lot. Sea-foam eyes and his personal opinion notwithstanding, he'd stay focused. He'd get some photos, write the report and collect his fee. The sooner he was out of the adultery business the better.

NEXT MORNING, Tyler found himself pulling right back into the Quayside parking lot. This time, Jenna was alone when she strode purposefully into the main foyer.

Looked like his first instinct had been right. Who went to the Quayside two days in a row? Who went there alone at this time of the morning, unless they were meeting somebody inside?

Tyler loved it when his instincts were firing on all cylinders. He pulled his baseball cap down low, donned dark sunglasses, grabbed his camera and followed her.

He pushed through the revolving glass door, glancing around the antique lobby until he spotted her near the concierge desk.

Perhaps somebody had left her a key with the concierge. Perhaps a young, virile somebody who would make her forget her fiancé for a couple of hours.

The concierge didn't hand her a key, but Jenna *did* pick up the house phone. Maybe luck was with him. Maybe young and virile would meet her right here in the lobby. Right here in camera range.

Though the light was bad, Tyler took a quick shot of Jenna talking on the phone.

Then he sidled over to a furniture grouping and eased down into a soft armchair. He wished he had another newspaper to hide behind, but he had to settle for the obscuring foliage of a large potted plant. He felt like a tacky Sam Spade, hovering, waiting, watching.

Jenna hung up the phone and moved away from the concierge desk, turning to face in his general direction. Her beauty rocked him back. For a minute, he almost wished he had a bank balance that would put him in the running to date her.

Angling his head, confident she couldn't tell the direction of his gaze through the tinted glasses, he looked his fill. Her thick, auburn hair bounced around her shoulders, setting off a creamy smooth complexion. Her lips were full, her cheekbones high and her skirted business suit showed off a figure that nipped and tucked in all the right places. He could sit here and watch her all day long.

He sighed. Too bad she was so willing to trade in those stunning looks for Brandon's money.

Something on the far side of the lobby caught her attention, and her amazing eyes lit up with recognition. Tyler gripped the camera as she smiled a greeting and started to walk toward an unseen person.

His gaze strayed to her silky legs. He'd always had a soft spot for shapely calves, especially those that rose so gracefully from strappy, feminine sandals. He felt a sudden burn in his chest at the thought of watching her greet a strange man with a squeeze and a kiss.

It got worse when he imagined those shapely calves doing...well, doing what shapely calves do when they don't have their stockings on. He ruthlessly tamped down the unruly image, sitting forward to peek around the edge of the plant.

Henry?

Gorgeous Jenna was here to cheat on rich Brandon

with Henry Wenchel? The scenario didn't bear thinking about.

This was way more information than Tyler wanted concerning his father's friend. And he couldn't help thinking that Henry's wife was *not* going to be happy.

Trying not to cringe, he quickly snapped a shot.

Henry reached out to briefly shake Jenna's hand. They spoke for a minute, keeping a respectful two feet apart. Henry talked and Jenna nodded. She smiled, but it wasn't an intimate smile, and neither of them made a beeline for the penthouse elevator.

Tyler tried not to feel too relieved. When he thought about it, if Henry was going to carry on an affair with a younger woman, he'd be pretty stupid to do it in his own hotel lobby in front of the security cameras.

A moment later, Jenna and Henry headed up the mezzanine stairs. Towards Henry's office. Henry's very public office. Tyler sighed, relieved that Jenna had legitimate business at the hotel. Even though it meant his instincts were malfunctioning again.

In HENRY WENCHEL'S OFFICE, Jenna sat very still and concentrated on not hyperventilating. He was taking out a pen. He was flipping to the back of the contract. He was touching the pen to the signature line. The pen was moving. He was signing.

Her heart rate increased, and she could feel her extremities start to tingle.

He was done.

He'd signed.

Henry Wenchel had just signed a contract to pay Canna Interiors an exorbitant sum for the preliminary designs. Preliminary designs which could lead to the interior decorating contract of a lifetime.

"Understanding the ambiance is so important, don't you think, Jenna?" He passed the contract across the table toward her and held out his gold pen.

"Yes." She nodded, taking a shaky breath. Her fingers were still tingling as she reached for his pen. She half expected to wake up any second.

"I hope a week away from home won't be too inconvenient for you."

Jenna slid the contract until it was directly below her, only half listening to Henry Wenchel. "A week?" she asked automatically.

There it was. A swoopy *H*, a pointy *W*, then a squiggle and a swirl and a dot. She suddenly wished she had a signature that looked more artistic than her plain old name. A signature that nobody could really read, because she was important enough that they'd all learned her squiggles.

"We'll assign you a suite," said Henry.

She touched the pen to the paper above the line that read *proponent*. "Suite?" Jenna asked as she wrote her first name.

"You'll stay here, of course, while you work."

The pen faltered on the *M*. Drat! The biggest signature of her life, and she couldn't even get the *M* right. She sure hoped that didn't void the contract.

She carefully finished McBride, then looked up at Henry. "Stay here?" she asked, blinking.

"The only way to get the true ambiance," Henry smiled. "That's not a problem is it?"

"No," Jenna hurriedly shook her head. She'd stay in Timbuktu if it made Henry happy.

"Perfect," said Henry. He pressed a button on the telephone console.

Jenna tried valiantly to look like she made deals of this magnitude every day of the week. If Henry could tell she was faking, he was certainly being polite about it.

"I'll put you in one of our executive suites," he continued. "They have a phone, fax, personal computer, printer, Internet access. If there's anything else you need, be sure to let Anna know."

Jenna nodded. She couldn't think of a single thing she could possibly need in life besides a plum contract and an executive suite at the Quayside.

Henry gestured toward the door. "Great. Let's go see a registration clerk."

Feeling like she was drifting through a dream, Jenna followed Henry back down the wide, curved staircase toward the reception desk. While they walked, she gazed at the marble pillars, the dome ceiling, the leaded windows. The carpets, wall coverings and furniture were aging, but the building itself was extraordinary.

"Hello, Tyler." Henry's hearty voice pulled her attention away from their surroundings.

A man standing at the reception desk turned abruptly, drawing back as if he was startled by the sight of them.

"What a coincidence." Henry clapped the man on the shoulder. "Tyler, I'd like you to meet Jenna McBride, our new decorator. Jenna this is Tyler—"

"Carter," the man inserted, holding out his hand.

Henry's eyebrows briefly knit together.

"I'm a security guard here at the hotel." Tyler Carter grasped Jenna's hand.

His hand was warm, his grip strong and his skin leathery enough to indicate he enjoyed some kind of outdoor sport. His dark glasses were perched on a straight nose, above a strong, square chin. The smile he flashed was friendly enough, but Jenna sensed some kind of tension behind it.

"Yes. Well." Henry cleared his throat. "We're just getting Jenna set up with a suite for the next week or so."

"Don't let me get in the way." Tyler gestured toward the receptionist and gallantly moved back.

HENRY WAS close on his heels as Tyler cut across the lobby. Meeting Jenna so soon wasn't exactly what he'd planned. But Tyler had to congratulate himself on coming up with the security guard cover story. Now he had an excuse to hang around the hotel. Even better, he had an excuse to snoop.

"Odd that I don't recall hiring another security

guard," said Henry as the distance between them and the reception desk increased.

"I'm undercover," said Tyler. "On a case."

"Somebody staying at the hotel?"

"As it turns out." He glanced back to where Jenna was checking in. A decorating job at the Quayside. Small world, but a convenient one.

"There's not a criminal in my hotel, is there?"

"Not a criminal." Still smarting from Derek's reaction to an adultery surveillance case, Tyler didn't jump to share the particulars with Henry.

"Are you planning to stay?" asked Henry.

"Stay?"

"For the undercover operation. Do you need a room?"

What a good idea. It would make snooping even easier. Besides, he was on a "money is no object" expense account. And it would sure keep Derek from worrying about where he was living.

"Sure. I'll take a room," said Tyler.

"Shall I put it on the Reeves-DuCarter account?"

Tyler grinned. "Bill IPS. I'm getting expenses on this."

"Good enough. You will let me know if my guests are in any danger?"

"That's a promise," said Tyler. Though it seemed unlikely that any of the guests could be decorated to death. He found his attention straying back to Jenna.

"What is Jenna McBride decorating?" he asked.

"She's giving the entire hotel a facelift." There was

some kind of a twinkle in Henry's eyes. "She came *very* highly recommended."

Tyler squinted at Henry's expression. It was sort of a wink, wink, nudge, nudge, inside joke expression.

Redecorating the hotel wasn't a bad idea. But Henry was sure acting strange about it. Maybe the older man did have a crush on Jenna.

If that was the case, Tyler could have told him that Jenna was already taken. He could also remind Henry that *Henry* was already taken.

Jenna started across the foyer toward them.

"Can you give me a security key?" asked Tyler.

"Not a problem." Henry nodded.

3

THE LIGHTHOUSE, the Quayside's rooftop seafood restaurant, wasn't light at all. Jenna squinted at the maitre d' as she took her seat at a small table in a secluded alcove. She supposed the darkness might seem romantic to some, but it was a crying shame to waste the view.

Although the restaurant was located on the fortieth floor, right on the lake front, only about a quarter of the exterior wall space had windows. The rest was covered in a heavy, burgundy wall paper, layered between dark, hewn beams.

The feeble ceiling lights cast a smoky, orange hue, and the carpet was in red tones. At least she thought it was in red tones, she leaned sideways in her seat and peered down at it. She could barely see her feet down there in the dark depths.

Glancing around to make sure nobody was paying attention, she lifted the candle from the middle of the table and held it close to the floor.

She was right. Swirls of burgundy and bloodred. She shuddered.

"Lose something, ma'am?"

Jenna quickly straightened in her chair, giving her emerald cocktail dress a surreptitious tug down her thighs and smoothing her fingertips across the straight, strapless neckline to make sure everything was where it ought to be.

"Nothing." She smiled at the waiter, placing the candle back on the table.

"Can I offer you a cocktail?" he asked, reaching out and returning the candle to its original position.

"Sure." Jenna tapped her fingernails against the gold tablecloth. "A glass of red wine?"

"We have the Andollin Beaujolais from France, very light, very smooth. Or the Posselini Merlot from Italy, bolder, very dry." He flipped open a leather-bound wine list. "Or I can open a bottle."

"The Beaujolais will be fine."

"Very good." He flipped the wine list shut. "I'll be back in one moment."

Jenna sighed and settled into her chair. The waiter's old-world mannerisms seemed to go with the room. Maybe wealthy people liked oppressive spaces and officious service. She'd certainly experienced both with Brandon.

Should she stay with dark and classic here, or be bold and suggest something more updated? She ran her fingertips along the ornate arm of the dark walnut chair, tracing the swirled carving as she gazed around the room, cataloguing the furniture and decor.

Most of the tables in her section were empty. Although, one of the window tables was occupied by a couple. She unconsciously paused on them. They were holding hands across the table top and seemed totally absorbed in each other, oblivious to anything else in the room.

After a brief twinge of envy, Jenna shifted her focus. It came to rest on the other chair at her table. The wood was dark, almost black, and the upholstery was diamond-tufted, red velvet. She imagined it had looked very rich in its time, but now it looked heavy and dated. Rather like the wallpaper.

Rather like the staff. She grinned to herself and took a quick sip from her water glass. She wondered if new uniforms would lighten them up a little.

Her gaze started to roam again, coming to rest on the couple by the window. The man reached into his suit pocket and pulled out a small, velvet box. Jenna's eyes widened along with the woman's, and Jenna quickly turned her head to look away.

She found herself focusing in on the wallpaper while she considered changing chairs so the couple wouldn't be in her line of vision. They obviously didn't need an audience tonight.

The wallpaper in front of her was starting to peel at one of the seams. For all its venerated reputation, the Quayside sure did need the services of a good decorator.

She touched the loose seam with her fingertip, and

pried away an inch of the brittle paper. It flaked off in her hand.

"Your wine, ma'am," the waiter startled her again, and she wondered if he practiced sneaking up on people.

"Thank you," she murmured.

"Are you ready to order?"

Jenna shook her head. "Not yet." She wasn't in a hurry.

As she sipped her wine, her attention kept wandering back to the wall beside her. Curious, she shifted in her seat, taking a closer look at the smooth, surface revealed under the wallpaper. It was drywall, probably put up in the sixties. And, since the hotel was more than fifty years old, that meant somebody had renovated the restaurant at least once.

She traced the seam partway up the wall, drawing closer. She pulled up on her knees, lifting the candle for a better look. If this was a renovation, what was the original design?

She glanced around the restaurant. Lattice dividers and carved, stone statues broke the large room into sections. Hers was definitely an outside wall. If the original designer had more brains than the renovator, there might be window openings back there. She felt a hum of excitement at the thought of more windows.

With all that light, all that view to play with, she could cheerfully blow the entire redecorating budget on the restaurant alone. The possibilities were positively endless.

She shimmied up higher. Glancing around to make sure the other two diners were still making moon eyes at each other and ignoring her, she knocked gently on the wall. It sounded solid. Drat.

She put the candle down and knocked again, a little to the left this time. Still solid. A statue kept her from trying further to the left, so she stretched up to reach above it, glancing at the other outside walls, counting off the windows and trying to eyeball the pattern. She reached up and knocked.

Hollow.

"Yes!" she whispered. Pay dirt.

She rapped her knuckles in a horizontal line, trying to ascertain the size of the opening. Then she went vertical, stretching up, standing in her seat. The hollow sound went up and up. Excitement hummed through her veins.

If the perimeter of the restaurant was all window openings, she was going to fill this mausoleum with light.

"Is something wrong?" A deep voice behind her startled her.

Jenna turned swiftly, bashing her shin against the tabletop, recognizing the security guard from the lobby earlier and knocking over the candle all in a split second.

"Ouch," she cried, leaning over quickly to blow out

the candle. Her breath bent the flame then, to her horror, it leapt higher, catching the wax-drenched tablecloth.

"Watch your hair," the man gasped, grabbing her around the waist and pulling her out of the chair. He held her tight with one arm, and swiftly snuffed the flame with his other palm.

But it didn't go out, and he jerked his hand back.

Panic surged in Jenna. Any second now the whole cloth was going to go up. The woman at the other table exclaimed and pointed.

Tyler grabbed Jenna's water glass and dumped it on the spreading flame. It hissed, and smoked, sputtering out, leaving a messy, saucer-sized black hole in the middle of the tablecloth.

"You okay?" Tyler asked in a deep voice that rumbled near her ear. His arm was still firmly around her waist.

"Fine," she answered, only slightly shaken. The throb on the front of her shin bone told her she'd have a bruise tomorrow. But no real damage had been done to the table, thank goodness.

"Thanks," she said.

"No problem," he replied.

The spilled water worked its way to the edge of the table and trickled onto the floor. Jenna picked up her napkin and began dabbing at the mess.

Tyler reached for the second napkin. He dropped

his arm from around her waist, but they were still shoulder to shoulder.

"Dare I ask?" He tipped his head to look at her as he blotted the water. His eyebrows quirked, and she found herself staring into the deepest, darkest, bluest eyes in the world. They were framed with thick, black lashes and shadowed by straight brows. Whoever decorated this guy had done a bang-up job.

"Ask what?" she managed as her pulse reacted to the fact that she was touching an extremely good-looking man. His biceps were rock hard, and his body heat radiated through his cotton shirt, warming her bare arm.

"Is everything all right here?" The waiter's voice interrupted. His words conveyed concern, but his expression was more exasperated than worried.

"We could use a new tablecloth," said Tyler evenly, dropping the wet napkin and guiding Jenna back a couple of steps. She didn't fight the continued body contact, since she kind of liked touching him.

"Of course," he finally said. He gathered Jenna's wineglass and the silver setting, then scooped up the tablecloth.

Tyler glanced back down at Jenna as the man walked away. A grin formed on his face, showing off the barest hint of a dimple. "Dare I ask what you're up to?"

"Experiencing the ambiance," she said, her shoulder still brushing against his arm. She should have felt crowded by his proximity in the small space, but it honestly felt flirty.

"Do you always stand on your chair to experience the ambiance?" His leg shifted, brushing once against her stockings, sending her nerve endings into a tizzy.

"Oh, that," she breathed, waving a hand toward the wall behind them. "I was just looking for windows."

His gaze shifted to the solid wall. "I hate to be the one to tell you this…" He turned the full force of his attention back to her, and she sucked in a tight breath.

From his tousled dark hair, to his devil-may-care smile, to his deep voice and broad shoulders, this guy was drop-dead sexy.

"I think they're behind the wall," she explained, struggling to understand her strong reaction to a virtual stranger.

"I take it you've got big plans for the place?"

"It's got loads of potential." She should move away now, break the subtle contact between their arms and sit back down. She really should.

He glanced around the restaurant. "Not a fan of early bordello?"

She smiled. That was *it*. The red velvet, the orange-toned lighting, the sultry feel of the atmosphere. Jenna could easily imagine Victorian era ladies of the evening plying their trade.

"Maybe the last decorator was trying for romantic?" she suggested charitably.

Tyler's expression turned skeptical.

"Sensual?"

"Sensual is free," he said. "When you pay for it, it's erotic."

Jenna bit down on the inside of her cheek. Nope, she didn't know this man. She wasn't going to make a risqué joke about his bordello experience.

He caught the look in her eyes. "The answer is never."

She shook her head, stifling a grin. "I never asked."

"Uh-huh." He shifted back, folding his arms. "But you were wondering."

She shook her head. "I'm only wondering how many windows are hidden behind the wall renovations." She kept a straight face for a moment before giving into temptation. "Of course, you *were* the one who recognized the bordello look right off."

"I've watched westerns."

"*Westerns?* Is that what they call them nowadays?"

His eyes turned to blue smoke, and he slowly took in her tight dress, stockings and high heels. "*Decorators?*" he drawled. "Is that what they call them nowadays?"

"Should I get out of this conversation while the getting is good?"

"Since we've both agreed we're standing in a bordello. And since you're the prettiest woman in the room. And since I'm about to make you an offer...

Yeah, we should both get out of this conversation before I get my face slapped."

"You couldn't afford me anyway," she boldly tossed out in a Mae West voice before stepping away from him and slipping into her chair.

He was silent for half a heartbeat as he took a seat across the table. Then his bass voice rolled. "Don't bet on it."

His dark eyes smoldered, and Jenna's entire body contracted.

Wow.

Nobody had ever looked at her like that before—sliding a white-hot gaze straight past her inhibitions.

"May I offer you a cocktail, sir?" The waiter interrupted, his formal tone almost icy. He stood to one side while a busboy swiftly replaced the tablecloth then set out silverware, menus and a new candle.

"Scotch," said Tyler, not appearing the least bit fazed by the waiter's tone. "Glenlochlan. And another glass of wine for the lady."

TYLER SETTLED BACK in the wide comfortable chair and watched the candlelight flicker on Jenna's flushed cheeks. She'd surprised him. Shocked the hell out of him, actually.

He'd been expecting a cold, brittle, uptight gold digger. What he got was a warm, funny, down-to-earth woman who could give as good as she got and was obviously serious about her business. Brandon was definitely getting his money's worth.

Her hair must have started the evening piled neatly on top of her head. But it was a little worse for wear now. Stray wisps teased her delicate ears and dangled around her square-cut emerald earrings.

The earrings matched the tight sheath of a dress she wore. It had probably started the evening a little higher and neater, too. Not that he minded. Not as long as they were hidden away in a dark corner where nobody else could get a glimpse of her cleavage.

A gentleman would tell her about her precarious hold on decency. Luckily, Tyler had never been a gentleman.

The waiter appeared and placed the scotch in front of Tyler and the wine in front of Jenna.

"Will you be placing your order now?" he asked, notepad at the ready, his dour expression aimed at Jenna.

Tyler hoped she'd hit him with a one-liner, but she bit her bottom lip guiltily and quickly reached for the menu.

Tyler placed a hand over hers. "Not quite yet," he said to the waiter, shooting him a warning look.

The man's attitude was making Jenna uncomfortable, and Tyler was not about to tolerate it. There was no excuse for treating a guest like you couldn't wait for them to leave. Especially one as sweet as Jenna.

Tyler weighed his options. He could burst the man's pretentious balloon with no more than a whisper of the Reeves-DuCarter family name. It turned waiters into scurrying little deferential peons.

For Jenna's sake, he was almost tempted.

Instead, he stood up and offered his hand. "Tyler Carter. Sorry for the inconvenience."

The man looked confused. He hesitantly reached out to shake Tyler's hand. "Uh, no trouble."

"Thanks for your help with the tablecloth." He gestured to Jenna. "We're going to enjoy our drinks, if you don't mind. We'll be ready to order a little later."

It was a dismissal. A polite one, but a definite one.

The waiter nodded, and started to withdraw. "Very good."

"Great." Tyler returned to his seat. He smiled at Jenna. "Just sit back and enjoy your wine."

She picked the glass up by its stem and gazed doubtfully at the ruby liquid. "I already drank most of the other one."

"So?" Wine loosened the tongue. Wine was an excellent beverage for a subject to drink.

Tyler forced himself to regroup. He couldn't forget why he was here, why he'd followed Jenna to the restaurant in the first place. Beautiful and charming as she was, this *wasn't* a date. And guilty as it was starting to make him feel, this *was* an interrogation.

"I'm working," she continued. "How am I going to

develop a color scheme for the restaurant if I'm drunk?"

"But how can you experience the true ambiance without wine?"

She laughed. It was a pretty laugh. Just like everything else about her.

"Were you by any chance a salesman in another life?"

"You mean in a Buddhist sort of way?"

"I mean in a 'buy the dicer-slicer in the next ten minutes and get the free Ginsu knives' sort of way."

Tyler chuckled. "Youngest child in the family. I had to learn to be charming to survive."

"Do you have brothers or sisters?" asked Jenna.

"Brothers. What about you? Your family live here in Seattle?"

She shook her head. "Minnesota."

"When did you leave Minnesota?" he probed.

"About five years ago. I won a scholarship to University of Boston."

That explained Boston. Didn't explain Brandon.

"So, why did you leave Boston?" Tyler knew the question should be what, or more importantly, *who* brought her to Seattle. But he was curious about Brandon, getting more curious by the minute, as a matter of fact.

Just how serious was this engagement from her perspective? She didn't wear a ring. Somehow, he'd expected a guy like Brandon to weigh her finger down with a carat or five.

Off topic, he warned himself. He was here working for Brandon, not against him.

"My business partner grew up in Seattle," she said. "We moved here a few months ago to open Canna Interiors."

Tyler watched her lips as she spoke. They glistened in the candlelight.

"Leave anyone behind?"

"What do you mean?"

"Boyfriend? Lover? Significant other?"

She stilled. "Why do you ask?"

Question with a question. He'd give her points for the evasive maneuver.

"You're a beautiful woman," he said.

She blushed, suddenly looking vulnerable. Her eyes widened and her lips softened.

His vision tunneled and all he could see were those lips. He was overwhelmed with the need to know their taste, their texture, their temperature.

He tossed back the scotch in a single swallow. "I somehow can't see all the men in Boston leaving you alone while you studied for your degree."

"There was nobody important in Boston," she said, glancing away, fidgeting with her glass.

It was a darn good thing she didn't make her living lying.

"What about a boyfriend in Seattle?" He watched her expression closely.

Tyler the P.I. wanted her to say yes and give him details. Tyler the man couldn't help wanting her to say no. Which was stupid, since boyfriend in Seattle or not, she still had a fiancé in Boston who was paying the bills.

She was unavailable, with a capital *UN*, and Tyler didn't know why he was deluding himself.

"No boyfriend," she said.

"Hmm-hmm." The waiter cleared his throat a discreet few feet away.

Tyler looked up.

"Another drink, sir?"

"We really should order." Jenna opened her menu.

He had to hand it to her. She knew just when to get the hell out of a conversation.

"HENRY SAID they were in the third drawer." The glow of the small desk lamp was the only source of light as Tyler sifted through a series of file folders in Henry's cabinet. He hadn't succeeded in getting any information from Jenna that would help his investigation, but he had called Henry as they left the restaurant. And, the evening wouldn't be a total loss if they found the old architectural drawings for Jenna.

Who was he kidding? Circumstances aside, he'd never classify an evening spent with a woman like Jenna as a loss of any kind.

"I can always get them in the morning," Jenna offered.

"We'll find them." Unfortunately the files were coded by number rather than common name.

"Want me to look for the light switch again?" she asked, leaning over his shoulder.

"It's probably on a timer," said Tyler, telling himself to concentrate on the search instead of her body heat. "The security guards probably control it from a central switch box."

"You don't know?" she asked.

Tyler paused. "I'm not usually on night duty."

"Oh."

He cursed under his breath. He couldn't forget about his cover like that.

"What's this?" She reached into the back of the drawer and pulled out a thick file.

"Could be it," said Tyler, stepping back, hoping a bit of physical distance would curb his desire.

Jenna turned to the desk. She opened up the folder. Sure enough, it was full of historic drawings.

The paper crackled as she carefully unfolded it on the desktop.

Tyler moved up beside her, aiming the lamp. "Look for the top floor."

"The lines are so pale, I can't tell what anything is," she sighed, smoothing the big sheets of paper against the oak desktop.

He reached in front of her and flipped a page.

"There's the lobby." He traced the line delineating the octagonal shaped room with his fingertip, pausing at the marble pillars one by one.

She was so close, he could almost bury his face in her hair. He inhaled deeply. Roses. He loved the smell of roses.

To distract himself, he turned another page. She moved unexpectedly and his biceps brushed the tip of her breast. "The pool," he gasped, pretending he didn't notice the touch, even as a burn of arousal invaded his system.

"What's that?" She pointed to a darkened square in the center of the page.

Had she noticed his inadvertent touch? She didn't react.

"The garden," he said.

"There's a garden in the middle of the hotel?" She glanced up at him.

"Yes. You access it from the spa." He looked down into her crystal green eyes. Bad move. They were way too close.

"This is very nice of you," she gave him a small smile, and his heart stopped beating.

"What's nice?" *She's engaged to your client, idiot.* His heart had no business doing anything strange in response to her smile.

"Tonight... Dinner..." She took a deep breath and tipped her head.

His heart slammed instantly into overdrive.

It was so wrong, but she was so close. All sweetness and light and softness. The slightest move on his part, and they'd be kissing. He'd be tasting her lips, exploring their tenderness, feeling their heat. Wet, wild and wonderful.

"Dinner was nice," he said instead, steeling his desire, threatening himself with dire consequences if he dared move even a centimeter closer.

"And you found the floor plans." She shifted, letting her thigh brush against his. She raised her hand to his biceps and rested her fingertips against his cotton sleeve.

Oh, no. That was an invitation only a total cad would ignore. He either had to kiss her now or insult her so bad.

Nobody said no to body language like that. Nobody said no to a woman who looked and smelled, sounded and felt like her.

"Jenna..." He needed to stop this. He needed to let her down easy.

"Yes?" she breathed.

He clenched his hands into fists, trying to get the right words, the right phrases to form in his mind. But, they didn't. There was no way out of this without kissing her.

Just quick, he promised himself. Just a brush. Just a taste.

He tipped forward.

Her eyes closed, and her lips softened.

Aw, hell. He gently pressed his lips against hers, promising himself he'd keep them closed, promising himself he wouldn't pucker.

Her hand convulsed around his arm.

A roar started in his ears and quickly overwhelmed his brain. His lips parted. She tasted of sweet wine and summer sunshine.

Her lips moved, and her breath sighed. And, for the life of him, he couldn't make himself let her go.

His hands crept up her back until they'd buried themselves in her thick hair, releasing the scent of roses and nearly blowing his mind.

Her lips opened wider, and he absolutely had to follow suit. He cupped the back of her neck, pulling her tighter. Want and need overwhelmed his system with the power of a midnight storm.

His knee slipped between her legs, and she pressed closer, her sweet body entwining itself with his own. He could feel himself slipping toward the point of no return.

He had to stop this.

Now.

Right now.

She was the subject of his investigation, for goodness sake. The fiancée of his client. He'd broken about a hundred ethical constraints already.

If he was ever going to look himself in the mirror again, he had to stop this right now.

He slowly pulled back. But her hand found its way

to the back of his neck. She pressed against him, coaxing him back down toward her mouth.

And he was tempted. If there was ever a moment to throw his principles to the wind, this was it.

"We can't," he choked out, resisting the pressure of her hand. "We *so* can't."

"What?" She blinked, eyes glazed and vulnerable.

"I'm sorry." He took a step away, gasping for breath, trying desperately to convince himself that the moral high ground was where he wanted to be.

He took another step back in case he weakened.

She tugged at her skirt, and he gritted his teeth.

"Are you married?" she asked, in a voice that sounded small in the empty office.

"No." He shook his head.

"Engaged?" She shifted beside the desk, casting shadows in front of the lamp.

"No."

She bit her lower lip. "Girlfriend?"

He shook his head again. He wanted to explain, but there was no way he could.

She laughed nervously, smoothing her hair back from her forehead. "Well. This is embarrassing." She started to move toward the door.

"Jenna."

She shook her head, without turning around. "Please, don't say a word. You'll only make it worse." She sounded like she meant it.

Tyler cursed under his breath.

He'd hurt her. He'd insulted her. She thought he didn't want her, when the truth was he wanted her so bad he could barely see straight. He opened his mouth, but there was no way to fix it.

She kept going.

He didn't stop her.

The door clicked firmly shut, and he swore out loud, banging the end of his fist against the desktop.

4

TYLER HAD TOSSED and turned in the king-size bed all
night long. Under other circumstances, he would
have kissed Jenna McBride and held her in his
arms—and whatever else she'd wanted—all night
long.

But these weren't other circumstances. She was the
subject of his investigation, and he was being paid by
her fiancé. That was about as off-limits as a woman
got.

He took a sip of his black coffee and flipped the
page of the newspaper he wasn't reading. At six-
thirty in the morning, there weren't many other hotel
guests in the main floor Cedar Room Restaurant, and
his lumberjack breakfast arrived quickly.

"Can I get you anything else?" asked the waitress
as she set down a plate filled with hotcakes, bacon
and scrambled eggs. She topped up his coffee.

He was hoping extra calories would make up for
the lack of sleep.

"I'm good." He gave her a smile, and she faded
back into the brightly lit, plant-filled room.

"Hey, little brother." Derek pulled out the chair across the table, surprising Tyler.

"What are you doing here?" Tyler quickly glanced at the entrance to the restaurant. Since Derek had checked out Jenna for him two days ago, the last thing Tyler needed was for her to see them together.

"Meeting with Henry." Derek reached out and snagged Tyler's untouched orange juice.

"Well, I'm working. And you'd better leave." Tyler took a first bite of the hotcakes and moaned in appreciation.

"Better than takeout, ain't it?" Derek smiled knowingly.

"Better than takeout," Tyler had to agree. "But get lost before Jenna sees you." He glanced at the entryway again. It was doubtful that Jenna would be up this early, but if she was, his cover could be blown in an instant.

"Jenna the cheating wife from Canna Interiors?"

"Fiancée."

"Why would she see me here?" asked Derek.

"She's staying here."

"Really?"

"Yes. Henry hired her to redecorate the place. He'll probably tell you all about it."

"You staying here, too?" Derek asked, reaching out for a slice of Tyler's toast.

Tyler rapped Derek's knuckles with his fork. "Yeah. I'm on an expense account."

"Great." Derek snagged the toast anyway. "This is much better than your office."

"I'm on a case. The subject stays here, I stay here."

"That's what I figured."

"What?"

"It makes sense." Derek's eyebrows rose. "Stay close to her, solve the case." He lifted the glass and swallowed the rest of the orange juice in one mouthful.

"Why, thank you for the vote of confidence. Now get out before you blow the entire thing." Tyler checked out the door once again to make sure Jenna hadn't made an appearance.

"No problem." Derek grabbed Tyler's second slice of toast and took a big bite. "Let me know if you need any more help."

"Just stay away from me so she doesn't connect us."

"Roger." Derek stood and gave Tyler a quick salute. "You sure I can't have a decoder ring?"

"Get out."

"Anything you want me to tell Henry?"

"Tell him not to forget my last name is Carter, and I'm his security guard."

Derek grinned. "Good cover. Catch her in a compromising situation yet?"

"Not yet." Not unless you counted the kiss in the office. But that was more of a compromise of Tyler's morals than of hers. Though, he had to admit, she sure hadn't acted like a happily engaged woman.

"Can I see the pictures when you do?"

"Not a chance."

If she'd kissed Tyler so willingly, who else would she kiss before the week was out? For some reason, the thought of catching her with another man made Tyler more angry than the thought of *not* catching her doing something he could report to Brandon Rice.

Which made no sense at all.

He needed the case over with, and he needed the money. The sooner the better.

"Spoilsport." Derek swiped the strawberry garnish from Tyler's plate and headed for the door.

"UNATTRACTIVE HOW?" Candice popped a plump berry into her mouth as they sat down at a small table in the Quayside lobby lounge. The breakfast buffet stretched for about a mile through the center of the casual table groupings beneath the domed, stained-glass ceiling.

"You know, not appealing," said Jenna.

"To who?"

"To men." Jenna dropped the linen napkin into her lap, slipped off her sandals and curled her legs beneath the plush armchair.

"You mean Brandon?"

"Of course not Brandon." Jenna tore her croissant

in half. Brandon definitely wasn't the cause of her ego bruising. She couldn't care less about Brandon.

Tyler, a virtual stranger, a man who'd apparently only been humoring her with that stupid kiss, had virtually obliterated Brandon from her mind.

"Then who?" asked Candice.

"Is this your roundabout way of agreeing that I'm not attractive?"

"Of course not. You're gorgeous. I'd kill to have hair that thick, and you'd stop traffic if you ever wore a miniskirt."

Jenna couldn't help but smile. She could always count on Candice. "Thank you."

"So, who sent your ego for a loop?"

"Does it have to be any one person in particular?"

Candice smiled, and tapped her polished index finger against her chin. "I guess not."

"Good," Jenna nodded, lifting her china coffee cup. Hopefully a decent shot of caffeine would make up for her lack of sleep last night. She needed to be *on* today.

"But, what did he do?" Candice leaned forward.

Jenna gave her head a little shake. If she really didn't want to talk about it, she shouldn't have brought it up in the first place. It was embarrassing, but Candice had already seen her at her worst.

"He kissed me," said Jenna, the words evoking a tactile, visual, flavored memory of Tyler's lips that made the blood roar through her veins even eight hours later. If he hadn't stopped...

"How horrible," Candice deadpanned. "I can see why you'd be questioning your desirability after an experience like that."

"And then he stopped," Jenna clarified.

"What do you mean stopped?"

"Stopped." She put her cup down. "One minute we were kissing, the next minute we weren't."

"You mean, all of a sudden like?" Candice leaned farther forward.

"Exactly."

"For no reason?"

"None at all."

"Were you alone?" Candice's eyes narrowed.

"Completely."

"Did you say no?"

Jenna shook her head, setting her cup back down in the gold rimmed saucer.

"Pull back? Gasp?"

"Only in delight."

"Who the hell are we talking about?"

"You don't know him."

"What do you think you're doing, kissing men that I don't know?" Candice spread her hands in mock horror.

A waitress paused to see if they needed anything. Candice smiled and shook her head.

"I would've called you while he was puckering,"

Jenna drawled. "But it was late, and I was worried it might spoil the mood." Not that the mood hadn't been torpedoed anyway.

"Well, next time plan ahead a little." Candice sniffed.

"Of course."

"And next time, find a guy with taste." She picked up her silver and cut into the mushroom omelette on her plate.

"What would turn you off?" asked Jenna. "If you were a guy, I mean? You think I came on too strong?"

She'd rather shamelessly shimmied up against him. And she'd wriggled her leg between his.

Jenna closed her eyes, feeling heat rush to her cheeks at the memory. It had been pretty brazen. But it had felt so right at the time.

He'd stared down at her with those smoky blue eyes, and she'd felt like the most desirable woman in the world. Could it have been an illusion?

"You? Come on too strong?" Candice shook her head. "I don't think so." She paused, and her eyebrows flexed. "What did you do?"

"Well. We were standing in—"

"Wait a minute. What is his name? What does he look like? If I'm going to picture this right, I need a visual."

"Tyler Carter. He's about six foot two, maybe six-three. Broad shoulders, dark hair, square chin. Kind of like..." she glanced around the room. "There. You remember Derek."

"Derek?" Candice's eyes widened and she blinked.

"The guy who gave us this job."

"Uh. Yeah. I remember him."

"He's standing right over there."

Candice swallowed. "Really?"

"Look."

Candice glanced cautiously to one side, then quickly turned her head back.

"Tyler looks a little like Derek. But not so overtly brawny."

"What's wrong with brawny?"

"Nothing's wrong with brawny. Did I say anything was wrong with brawny?"

"No." Candice straightened in her chair. "But you compared Tyler with Derek. And, since you obviously think Tyler is hot then, implicitly, Derek isn't."

Jenna stared at her friend. "Huh?"

"Never mind." Candice picked up her coffee cup and took a drink.

"Okay. Wait a minute. He's coming over."

"Who?" Candice paled.

"Derek." Jenna lifted her napkin from her lap and eased her feet back into her sandals.

"Hi, Derek." She stood up and offered him her hand. "Did Henry Wenchel tell you he offered us the contract?"

"I met with him this morning."

"You remember my partner, Candice," Jenna nodded in Candice's direction.

Derek looked at her. His forehead furrowed.

Candice stood up, and Jenna could see the tension in her posture.

"We met the day before yesterday in our offices," she said.

"Ah," Derek nodded, holding out his hand. "I remember now."

Jenna watched the exchange with interest. Many were the times men forgot about Jenna when Candice was in the room. But it had sure never happened the other way around.

"How is the contract working out?" he asked Jenna. "Is the suite all right?"

"The suite's fine."

Candice plunked back down in her chair, a look of resignation crossing her face.

"Would you care to join us?" asked Jenna. Derek could very well be Henry Wenchel's boss. For all Jenna knew, he was the man who would make the final decisions on the designs.

Derek glanced quickly around the lobby. "Better not. I've got a meeting."

Just then, Jenna spotted Tyler coming down the mezzanine stairs. He glanced at Jenna. His gaze darted to Candice and Derek. Then it snapped back to Jenna.

His eyes widened in panic and he took an abrupt left turn in the direction of the spa.

Well. She supposed that answered any lingering illusions she might have had that he'd regretted backing off last night.

"I'm not in the hotel very often," said Derek. "But I might run into you again later in the week."

He turned to Candice. "Nice to see you again."

"Sure." She nodded.

"Goodbye, Derek," said Jenna.

As he walked away, Jenna dropped back down in her seat. "He's married," she said.

"Derek?"

"Tyler."

"The kissing-stopping guy?"

"Yeah."

"How would you know that?"

"I just saw him."

"Where?" Candice craned her neck to look around the lobby.

Jenna shook her head. "He's gone. Took one look at me and couldn't race out of here fast enough."

"Hmmm," said Candice, tapping her fingertip against the handle of her fork. "That definitely sounds suspicious."

"Doesn't it, though?"

"You're better off without him. After all, all you invested was one little kiss."

Actually, it was two. Or was it three? How could a

woman count a thing like that when one passionate experience blended right into the other with barely a breath in between. Barely a breath. Barely a murmur. Barely a centimeter between her and paradise.

TYLER DIDN'T STOP walking until he was almost to the conference center. Here, the hallway widened into another lobby in the new wing of the hotel which serviced business conventions.

He pulled his cell phone out of his jacket pocket and dialed Derek's cell number.

"Reeves, here," Derek answered.

"Step away from the table," Tyler growled.

"Hey, Tyler. What's up?"

"Do *not* use my name."

"Why not? Tyler Reeves—"

"Shut—"

"—private investigator—"

"—up."

"—working undercover as a security guard," Derek practically sang.

"All right. Where are you?" Tyler slumped against the lobby wall.

"Outside in the parking lot, just heading for my car."

"What were you doing talking to Jenna?" Tyler wanted to talk to Jenna. He needed to talk to Jenna and explain why he'd stopped them last night.

Not that he could really explain. But he sure

couldn't let her think it was something she'd done. He hadn't come up with a plausible story yet. But he definitely intended to.

"They spotted me in the lobby. I couldn't very well ignore them. They think I'm a potential client."

"Is that what you told them?"

"Of course that's what I told them. You thought I'd just wander into their offices and ask to use the restroom or something?"

"What do they think you're decorating?"

There was a pause on the line. "Sorry. Lost you there for a second," said Derek. "What did you say?"

"What did you tell them you wanted to redecorate?"

"My house."

"Well, just stay out of my way for a week. Your part of the case is finished." Tyler pushed away from the wall and started back toward the main lobby. He wanted to pick up Jenna's trail before she left.

"No can do, Tyler."

"Why not?"

"I'm taking a more hands-on approach with the hotel."

"Is there a problem?"

"Dad just asked me to give Henry a hand."

And what Dad wanted, Dad got.

"Avoid Jenna," said Tyler. "I don't want her to see us together." The number of people in the hallway increased, as did the noise level as Tyler grew closer to the main lobby.

"What? You're worried I'll slip up and call you bro' in front of her?"

"I don't know what you'll do."

"Battery's low, bro'. Better sign off."

The line clicked in Tyler's ear as he rounded the corner to the lobby and glanced around for Jenna.

First, he had to make up for his cloddish behavior. Then he had to figure out how to word his progress report to Brandon.

5

JENNA CURLED UP on one of the couches in the tea-room next to the spa, her sketch pad in hand. Through the glass wall, she could see people working out on the equipment and lounging in the whirlpools. Over her shoulder, the sun was setting across Lake Washington.

Gradual, full spectrum lighting would help make the transition from daytime to night smoother in the facility. She made a note of that.

She'd also discovered that the pool tiles could stand replacing. But, new tiles would cost an exorbitant amount of money. She settled for sketching in some additional windows and skylights, new furniture and a revamped shower area. That, along with a change in color scheme, would bring the spa up to date.

She reached for her steaming cup of herb tea. Dinner in the Lighthouse Restaurant was next on her agenda. It had been a struggle to avoid the memories of Tyler—and Tyler himself. But, at least she now had a good handle on the lobby and the guest rooms. And the convention center wasn't going to need any immediate attention. It was less than five years old.

She had no more excuses for putting off the restaurant visit. It was going to be her biggest challenge. She needed to find a way to totally change the atmosphere without exceeding the annual operating budget of a small country.

When the waiter came by offering her more tea, she shook her head. The spa was starting to clear out, most people heading out for dinner or the evening. Which was what she had to do.

If only she could find a way to keep the memories of Tyler at bay, so she could concentrate on her work.

Her ego was recovering. At least she thought her ego was recovering. Yesterday, when Candice had stopped in for a quick lunch between final crises on the hospital project, she'd pointed out several gentlemen giving Jenna appreciate looks.

It helped to know she wasn't totally unappealing to the opposite sex. Maybe she was just a lousy kisser.

Heaven knew, Brandon hadn't been big on kissing. He didn't like public displays of affection, and he was nothing if not efficient about the private displays.

Maybe it was a lack of practice. Though, exactly how a twenty-six-year-old woman gained kissing practice without making a complete fool of herself was beyond Jenna.

She hadn't seen Tyler since that morning in the lobby when he'd practically run away at the sight of her. And it wasn't like she could track him down and ask him what she'd done wrong.

Unless he really was married.

No. Upon further analysis, she'd remembered asking him point-blank. And if he'd been breaking away from their kiss because of his wife, there was no reason for him to lie. Men lied about their marital status to *get* another woman into bed, not to avoid it.

Which left her back at square one with being a really lousy kisser.

"Ma'am?" one of the waiters asked softly.

Jenna looked up.

"We're about to close."

"Oh." She scrambled to stand up. "I'm sorry."

"No problem." He smiled, forestalling her with a raised palm. "I know you're the decorator. You're welcome to stay as long as you like. If you leave through the main spa door," he pointed across the room, "the night security lock will engage automatically behind you."

"Thanks," Jenna nodded. She couldn't quite bring herself to face the memories of Tyler in the Lighthouse Restaurant yet.

"No problem. Mr. Wenchel asked us to give you our full cooperation."

As the door clicked shut behind the last staff member, Jenna stood up. The lights in the spa were dim now, and the whirlpool motors droned quietly on low speed.

She kicked off her sandals. Then, with a quick glance around to make sure she was completely alone, she slipped off her stockings as well.

Leaving her teacup and her sketch pad behind, she padded off the wooden floor of the tearoom onto the cool tiles of the spa.

She paused, dipping her toe into one of the whirlpools. The effervescent water tickled in a sensual sort of way.

She dipped a bit further, stretching out her arch in the warm water. Whether from Tyler's kiss or just coincidence, her hormones had been revving on high for the past few days.

She loosened her braid, shook out her hair, tipped her head back and closed her eyes. The swirling tickling water beckoned.

Resting her foot on the top step, she lowered herself onto the edge of the small pool, easing her other foot into the water, rubbing her toes against one another. She shimmied, pulling the bottom of her dress above her panties to make sure it didn't get wet.

The swirling water raised goose bumps. She stretched out her legs, but that wasn't enough. She wanted to strip off her clothes and enjoy the sensual feel of the water against her entire body.

She glanced at the spa door. While she worried her lower lip, trying to decide just how brave she was feeling, her gaze came to rest on the smallest of the whirlpools. It was off in a corner, partially concealed by the divider of rattan and vines.

She gauged the angle between it and the door.

If somebody did come in, she could throw her dress back on before they had a chance to see her.

Jenna stood up.

The rough tile scraped against her warmed, sensitized feet as she crossed to the little pool. The ventilation fans whirled, undulating the delicate leaves on the fig trees which lined the wide windows. A light floral perfume covered the chemical smell of the pools, and muted light shimmered on the surface of the water.

Before she had a chance to change her mind, she boldly stripped off her panties and pulled her knit dress over her head. Naked, she shivered, not quite believing she was actually going to do this.

Then she stepped into the pool and sighed as the warm water engulfed her calves. Her tongue moistened her lips. The soft water tickled the backs of her knees. Then slipped slowly, erotically up the length of her thighs, warm, wet, motion.

She bit back a moan.

The latch on the front door clicked, the ominous sound echoing through the cavernous room.

Jenna gasped, scrambling out of the whirlpool, water dripping down her legs, stretching for her dress.

The door hinges groaned as she yanked the black knit garment over her head.

They groaned again, swinging back to snap shut.

Jenna jerked the fabric down over her wet thighs. There wasn't time to do anything about her panties, so she tossed them behind one of the potted palm trees.

Her skin was flushed, her heart pounding, and remnants of the erotic experience pulsed through her veins.

"Jenna?"

Her eyes widened at the sound of Tyler's voice.

"Henry said you were in here," Tyler called.

"I'm...uh...just..." She frantically smoothed the wrinkles out of her dress and pushed her loose, steam-damp hair back from her forehead.

"Where are you?" he called.

"Back...uh..." She stepped out from behind the rattan screen. "Just dunking my feet." She tried to keep the guilt out of her voice. After all, it was none of his business if she wanted to dunk her feet, or her legs, or anything else for that matter.

"I wanted to talk to you." He moved closer, focusing on her location.

"About?" She stayed still. Her legs were starting to feel like jelly, and she wasn't sure if she could move them.

"I wanted to apologize." He came to a halt in front of her, all height and strength, square chin and probing blue eyes.

For a guy who didn't find her attractive, there was

sure a whole lot of intensity in his expression. His gaze was hotter than hot as it traveled from her damp hair to her bare feet. Or maybe it was just her imagination and the eroticism left over from her brief skinny-dip.

"I wanted to apologize," said Tyler, his gaze returning to her face. He looked genuinely regretful.

"About what?" She pretended not to understand. Maybe if she treated the whole kiss casually, he'd figure that it meant nothing to her. That he didn't have the power to crush her ego and self-confidence in one fell swoop.

He eased in closer, making her heart rate increase, bringing her buzz of arousal to a frustrating crescendo.

"It's not that I'm not attracted to you."

"Right." She dredged up the sarcasm from somewhere deep inside. Thank goodness she still had a glimmer of a self-protective instinct.

"You are a stunningly attractive woman."

"Why, thank you," she said tartly, making to step around him, wanting nothing more than to get away from her contradictory feelings of arousal and annoyance. If only he'd given her five more minutes in the hot tub, this flushed feeling of desperation would be long gone.

"Jenna." He gently touched her arm, and the sensation of the hot tub bubbles paled in comparison. "Please don't."

"Don't what." Her voice had taken on a breathless quality. Which was no wonder—because she couldn't actually breathe at the moment. She stopped.

"Don't walk away." He angled his body so that they were face to face. His dark blue eyes smoldered.

The perfumed air burst into a million fragrance streams, and the sound of the pool motors roared in her ears.

"Why?" If he didn't want to kiss her, why was he looking at her like that? Why was he asking her to stay? Why was he bending low, lips parting, whispering her name...

THE TASTE of Jenna rocketed through Tyler's system.

He'd spent the last two nights fantasizing about her, but his imaginings paled in comparison to the real thing.

He wrapped his arms around her and pulled her close, pressing her curves against his body. He wished he wasn't wearing a suit. The fabric was too thick, the cut too stiff, he wanted to feel every curve and hollow of her body beneath that clingy little dress.

She softened and moved in closer, arms twining around his neck, legs brushing against his, her fingertips finding the soft hairs at the base of his scalp.

He let his tongue roam free, and she opened wider, welcoming him, tangling with him, turning his muscles to tempered steel with her throaty murmurs.

He kissed her cheek, moving to her temple, testing the softness of her neck as his fingers tunneled into her hair. She was all softness and malleability. The scent of her wildflower perfume surrounded him, hijacking reason, propriety and common sense.

He wanted her so badly, he thought his body might snap from the strain.

How the hell had he ever walked away?

He pushed the cap sleeve down, tracing the tip of her shoulder with his tongue, and planting exploratory kisses along the length.

Her hands moved to his biceps, gripping tight, anchoring herself through the thick fabric of his suit. He had to get rid of the stupid suit.

But first, he wanted to do something about her clothes.

Her head tipped back, and he pushed her sleeve further down her arm. The neckline tightened over the mounds of her breasts.

He checked the progress, dragging the fabric ever so slowly across her taut breasts. Her eyes pinched shut, and she gasped as her coral nipples popped out. He swallowed, staring at their perfection for as long as he could stand.

Then he bent his head, taking one hard pebble into his mouth.

He wrapped his forearm around the small of her back, holding tight, balancing her, pressing one thigh between her legs as a kaleidoscope of colors burst free in his brain.

She whispered his name over and over.

He changed directions and with the fabric from the bottom of her dress fisted in his hands, drew the garment up over her buttocks, reeling, twirling, pulling. When his thumb touched skin, and he realized she wasn't wearing panties, he let out a guttural groan.

He pulled her flush against him, wrapping his arms tight around her, kissing her ear, her hair, her temple.

He cracked his eyelids, and a funny red light broke through the laser show going on in his brain.

He blinked.

He focused.

He swore.

"What?" Her voice was shaky.

Tyler quickly jerked down the back of her dress. He broke away and tugged at her neckline, settling it back into place.

"Tyler?" She blinked in confusion, stumbling as he let go of her.

He quickly grabbed her by the upper arms to make sure she didn't fall.

"I have to..." Oh, man. How on earth could he do this again? "I'm sorry."

Her eyes narrowed. They hardened. "You're leaving?"

"It's..." How could he tell her? How could he not?

There was a security camera staring him right in the face.

They'd captured everything. His kisses, her breasts, her thighs, her buttocks.

How on earth was he supposed to tell a woman they'd possibly just put on a show for the nightshift up in the control center? And there'd be a tape.

"I'm *so* sorry." He shook his head, backing away. "There's something I have to—"

"Are you *sick?*" She stared at him in absolute disgust.

All he could do was shake his head. "I have to go." He edged toward the door. If nobody was manning the camera, maybe he could destroy the tape. Maybe he could make it into the security control area and steal the surveillance tape and save Jenna's dignity. But it had to be done right now.

"Is this some kind of game?" she asked.

"No game." This was the most horrible thing he'd ever done in his life. He'd hurt her again. He'd insulted her. But there was no way he was going to tell her about the camera. Not until he found out if he could fix it.

"You get your jollies by turning women on and then backing away?" She marched toward the tea-room and scooped a sketch pad off the table. "I can't believe I fell for it a second time."

"Jenna." He wanted so badly to stay with her. But

he couldn't afford to waste a minute. "I'll talk to you later."

"I don't think so." She headed for the door. "In fact, I'd appreciate never seeing you again, Tyler."

"Jenna."

The door slammed.

Tyler's shoulders slumped, and he shook his head, allowing himself to wallow in self-pity for about thirty seconds. As soon as he figured Jenna had made the lobby, he sprinted for the service elevator.

THANK GOODNESS Henry had given him a security key.

Tyler looked both ways along the third floor hallway before slipping his key into the lock of the solid door. He had no idea what he was going to do if he opened it to a roomful of leering men.

He turned the handle and heard a muted click. He pushed slowly, revealing a dim room with banks of computers and electronic equipment around the edges. No security guards.

He breathed a sigh of relief and slipped inside.

The only light came from the computer screens and the white and green operation lights that blinked on and off behind glass panels.

Tyler rolled a chair over to the security camera monitors. There were several for the lobby, more in the convention center, the restaurant, and the spa.

There was a bank of videotapes behind the monitors, connected by wire to the CPU. But the glass cover was locked and none of the tape ports were labeled.

He picked up the phone and dialed Derek's cell. Derek was by far the family member most involved in the hotel on a day-to-day basis. He was also president of the Reeves-DuCarter electronics division.

"Reeves here."

Thank goodness. "It's Tyler."

"What's up at the hotel?" asked Derek.

"I need your help."

Derek's tone turned serious. "Be there in five minutes."

"No." Tyler squeezed his eyes shut. "You don't have to come. I just need to know about the security cameras."

"What about them?"

"How can I tell which tape goes with which camera?"

"Why?"

Tyler paused. "I need to get a tape."

"What happened? You steal something?"

"No."

"You want it for the investigation."

"Yeah." In a manner of speaking.

"Catch the cheating wife in the act."

"No! She's not his wife. She's his fiancée." A very important distinction to Tyler at the moment.

"I'm turning into the parking lot," said Derek.

"I told you, you don't need to come."

"Yes, I do. I can't figure this out over the phone. I need to look at the equipment."

"You sure?"

"Of course I'm sure. What's the big deal? We'll check out the tapes and find the right one."

"Sure." Tyler tried to sound nonchalant about it. But there was no way in hell his brother was getting a look at that tape.

"I'm in the lobby," said Derek.

"Don't let anyone see you come up here," Tyler warned.

"When will my decoder ring be ready?"

Tyler hung up the phone. He leaned forward and rested his elbows on the desktop, cradling his forehead.

What on earth did Jenna think of him right now?

Stupid question. He knew exactly what she was thinking. She thought that he was some sicko freak who got his thrills by teasing women.

If she only knew how it killed him to leave her.

Well, when he got his hands on the tape, she was going to know.

As long as he had the only copy, and there was no danger that the tape would entertain the security staff, he was going to tell her exactly why he'd backed off a second time. He'd make her understand that it wasn't *anything* to do with her desirability.

The door opened, and Derek slipped into the office.

"No tail on me," he stage-whispered with a grin.

"Just tell me which tape to destroy."

"Why would you want to destroy it?" Derek started across the room. "I thought it was going to be evidence for your case."

"Right," said Tyler. "That's what I meant."

Derek looked at him strangely. Then he turned his attention to the bank of videotapes.

"Let's see." He pulled out a ring of keys. "I think this one opens the lock box."

He crossed the room and opened a metal case. The doors of the case were lined with row upon row of keys.

"Mechanical," Derek read. "Electrical, housekeeping, concierge, main desk."

Tyler's foot tapped as he waited for Derek to find the right keys. He glanced from the door to the videotapes to the clock. Nine-fifteen. If they hurried, he could catch Jenna before she went to bed tonight.

"Security," said Derek, a triumphant note in his voice. "Now we just need to find the right one for the video cabinet."

Tyler stood up and paced across the office. He laced his fingers together and stretched them out in front of him. Then he tipped his head back and forth, trying to relieve some of the tension in his neck.

"Something wrong?" asked Derek.

"Nope."

"You're acting like a flea on a scratching dog."

"I'm fine."

"Here we go." Derek held up a key.

The knob on the office door rattled.

Tyler jumped to one side, flattening himself against the wall.

Derek looked at him like he'd gone crazy.

The door swung open, but Tyler stayed hidden behind it.

"Hey, Cory," said Derek, nodding to the unseen man.

"Oh. Hi, Derek. It's you. Everything all right?"

"It's great. I'm just running a couple of A/V tests before the bankers' convention tomorrow. How are Lisa and the kids?"

"They're fine," said Cory. "Let me know if you need any help."

"Will do," said Derek. "Can you make sure the projectors are operational in the executive boardrooms?"

"You got it," said Cory, pulling the door closed.

Derek pasted Tyler with a narrow-eyed look. "What the hell is going on?"

"Nothing," said Tyler.

"You sure this tape's not going to show you committing a crime?"

"I'm sure." It wasn't illegal to kiss a woman, or to do more than kiss her. Even if she was engaged.

Derek shook his head, returning to the keys and video cabinet.

He inserted the key. "Which tape are we looking for?"

"The spa," said Tyler.

"We're going to have to check them all. I have no idea which one covers which area." Derek sat down at a computer terminal and punched in a few keys. "I'll just pause the program."

A blue screen came up, and Derek punched a few more keys. "You realize this is only legit because we're manually monitoring right now. So, keep an eye on the lobby."

"Right." Tyler glanced at the screen which showed the main lobby. Everything looked normal.

"Start at the top," Derek muttered, pulling out the first of twenty tapes.

He slid across the room on the wheeled chair and popped the tape into a VCR. He rewound a few minutes and they started to view.

Tyler took a deep breath as the conference center came up on the screen.

"Next," said Derek, wheeling back.

Tyler glanced at the active monitors, leaning back against the desk, gripping the lip with sweating fingers as Derek moved back and forth.

"Bingo," Derek muttered on tape number five. The empty spa came up before them.

"Great," said Tyler. "Give me that one."

"Not so fast."

"No!" Tyler sprang forward.

Derek put out an arm and physically stopped him.

Before Tyler could break free of his brother's hold, Derek hit the play button.

Tyler swore colorfully as an image of him kissing Jenna appeared on the screen.

"Turn it off," he demanded through clenched teeth.

"Well, well, well," Derek drawled. "We do have videotape of the fiancée and another man." He whistled between his teeth.

With a burst of strength, Tyler yanked his brother's arm out of the way and hit the stop button.

Derek crossed his arms and swiveled the chair until he was facing Tyler. "Care to explain?"

"I kissed her," said Tyler.

"Kissed her?"

Tyler nodded sharply.

"Yeah. Right. That's why you were ready to break my arm to stop the tape."

"Okay." Tyler hit the eject button. "There was some skin. She's a nice woman, and I don't want you or anybody else ogling her."

"Except you."

"It didn't go much past a kiss." Tape securely in his hand, Tyler backed away.

Derek scooted back to the desk and opened a drawer. "Are you going to use it in the investigation?"

"Of course not."

He removed a new tape and filled the empty slot. "Seems to me you could wrap this up pretty quick. You just phone up Brandon what's-his-name and tell him he's right. His fiancée's fooling around. With the private eye."

Tyler blew out a hard sigh. "And give up the money."

He'd love to give up the money—dearly love to give up the money. But that would mean giving up his business and his independence. And, he'd spent too much of his life fighting to get where he was today.

Even if Jenna was the prettiest, sweetest, best kisser he'd ever come across, he had to see this through. He had to recover from this financial setback on his own if he wanted to hang on to his pride.

"I'll lend you the money." Derek locked the cabinet.

Tyler shook his head. "I'll give him a report. I won't use any names. What he does after that is his business."

"He'll dump her."

"He doesn't deserve her."

"And you do?"

Tyler paced across the room, running his hand through his short hair. Whether or not he deserved Jenna wasn't the point. "All I did was kiss her."

"Then why won't you let me see the tape?"

"Her dress slipped down."

"Slipped?" Derek's eyebrows jumped.

"Yes. *Slipped*. Now, don't you get all judgmental on me."

"I'm not judgmental," Derek denied.

"I know what I'm doing, and I don't need your help." Tyler knew that Derek was no saint.

Jenna *wasn't* married. She was engaged. And she still had plenty of time to change her mind about Brandon. In fact, if Brandon broke it off, it would probably be the best thing that ever happened to her.

Tyler would file an honest report. He'd simply decline to name the gentleman involved. That wasn't so unusual. Perfectly normal.

"Whatever you say." Derek returned the key and secured the lock box. "Just stay away from the security cameras next time."

Tyler's hand tightened around the tape. He definitely intended to.

6

JENNA SQUEEZED her hands together, trying to contain her excitement while Henry Wenchel, the hotel manager, perused the collection of decorating sketches scattered across the boardroom table. Here they were after four days and many hours of hard work. The muted sounds of telephones, computer printers and disjointed business conversations floated in from the outer office.

Tyler had left her several messages on her voice mail, but she'd deleted them all, forcing her mind away from the embarrassment of their last encounter. And, for the most part she'd succeeded. Now, she tried to appear calm and professional, but her anticipation was mounting as she waited for Henry to speak. She was proud of the ideas she'd submitted, and she couldn't wait to talk about them in more detail.

It had been a difficult proposal to put together. Battling anger and humiliation over Tyler, it had taken her a full twenty-four hours before she'd worked up the nerve to return to the Lighthouse Restaurant.

But, to her professional credit, she had returned.

She'd conquered the confusing memories, and carried on with the job.

Once she'd made it past the Tyler factor—at least during the daylight hours—her excitement over the project grew.

As a young girl, she'd used simple practical things to pretty up the family's austere farmhouse. Then, as a university student, she'd haunted yard sales and junk stores looking for just the right pieces to refinish and add to her small apartment. The results were all the more gratifying because she used ingenuity instead of money.

Henry cleared his throat, and Jenna sat up straighter, her professional smile helped along by the glow of her inner thoughts.

"Well," said Henry. "These are..." He shuffled the pile into order again, brow furrowing.

Jenna's smile faltered. Was something wrong?

"I think maybe I wasn't clear in my instructions."

Not clear? As in, she'd gotten it wrong? Jenna's gaze flew to the sketches, heart sinking.

He stood up, crossed the room and closed the boardroom door. The noise from the outer office immediately ceased, replaced by an ominous quiet.

When he turned back to face her, his expression was grave.

Jenna could hear her heart beating, her breathing, the clock in the corner ticking off the tense seconds.

Henry didn't like the sketches.

He was going to cancel the contract.

She closed her eyes for a second, dread filling her.

She'd been a fool to put the sketches forward without Candice's final okay.

But, Candice had been so busy at the hospital. And Jenna had been so confident of her work. And she'd wanted so badly to surprise her partner.

And, now, she'd blown the entire contract.

"I should have made it clear," said Henry, moving to the table and resuming his seat. "This is a serious renovation."

And Canna Interiors had not yet risen to the level of a serious firm. She should have known they couldn't compete at this level this soon.

"You've done a competent job within the confines you've set for yourself."

Competent. Damned with faint praise.

She swallowed around her dry vocal chords. "Confines?" she rasped.

"I'll be frank," said Henry.

Jenna wasn't sure she was ready for frank.

"We're looking for a visionary on this job."

His words pricked her pride. She'd always pictured herself as a visionary. From the time she was five years old, she'd imagined she could work miracles. A curtain here, a picture there, new surroundings for the doll who sat on the lace doily her grandmother had made.

Every morning, throughout the warm months,

Jenna would get up early to gather flowers for the scarred wooden table in the middle of the kitchen. Nobody thanked her, but she knew her father liked them by the way he smiled.

"Do you understand the phrase 'money is no object'?" asked Henry.

Jenna slowly nodded. It wasn't exactly within the realm of her experience, but she knew it was a far cry from cutting up rags for doll clothes and putting wildflowers in jelly jars.

He smiled kindly. "I mean really understand it? Your ideas will costs hundreds of thousands of dollars."

Jenna nodded again. Her ideas weren't exactly cheap, but she didn't think they were too outrageous.

"The Quayside board is prepared to spend millions."

Jenna blinked, sitting back in her chair. "Millions?"

Henry nodded. He waved dismissively at the drawings she'd worked so hard on. "A coat of paint and a new love seat aren't going to do it."

In the silence that followed, Jenna shakily stood up and began gathering the drawings.

So much for bringing beauty to the Quayside.

So much for impressing Candice.

She'd done her best, and it wasn't good enough.

"We have two more days before the quarterly board meeting," Henry went on. "Can you bring me something different?"

Jenna swallowed and nodded. Two days to totally rethink her ideas? Two days to make her instincts mesh with Henry's money-is-no-object vision?

She could try.

"Remember," said Henry, his voice still kind. "Think big. Think innovative. Think five star."

"I will," Jenna said as bravely as she could, wanting nothing more than to run away and hide.

TYLER HAD BEEN on the lookout for Jenna for the past two days, hoping for a chance to apologize and explain his reaction in the spa. But he had other cases on his plate, and he couldn't spend every waking minute at the Quayside.

He'd caught a glimpse of her in the lobby once, and he was pretty sure he'd spotted her in the convention center yesterday. But, both times, she'd disappeared before he could reach her.

He'd also called her room numerous times. Either she wasn't picking up, or she wasn't spending much time there. He'd considered using his pass key and some trumped-up excuse to let himself inside. But, even with the newly discovered flexibility in his ethics, he couldn't bring himself to invade her privacy.

He came around the corner hallway into the Lighthouse Restaurant—the last stop on his most recent methodical search of the building. This was getting pathetic. He was going to have to turn in his P.I.

license soon if he couldn't find one lone woman within the confines of a hotel.

She had to be *somewhere.*

"I'm sorry, sir." A tuxedoed waiter appeared in the restaurant foyer, putting up a hand to forestall Tyler's progress. "We're closed until six."

"I'm Tyler Reeves-DuCarter," said Tyler. For once not even flinching as he shamelessly dropped the family name.

"Oh." The waiter paused. Then he took a step back and gave Tyler a nod. "Of course."

Tyler thanked the man before proceeding, telling himself the name was nothing. It wasn't like he'd used the family name for personal gain. He needed to find Jenna. For her sake more than his.

Definitely for her sake.

The restaurant was horseshoe-shaped around a big, leather and mahogany bar that curved in front of the kitchen. Tyler worked his way around, progressing toward the back corner where he'd met Jenna on that first night.

The memories of their dinner together were still fresh in his mind. Without half trying, he could recall every word she'd spoken, every nuance of her expression. Before he'd insulted her in Henry's office, she'd been lively, open, funny and beautiful.

Somehow, some way, he knew he needed to get their relationship back on track. Although, as a starting point, he'd settle for simply finding her.

As he rounded the last corner in the room, he spotted her. A burst of relief shot through him, and he felt forty-eight hours of tension drain out of his body.

She was curled up in a corner table by the window. Her shoes were under the table, her sketch pad was in her lap, and the floor around her was littered with crumpled paper.

As he drew closer, he could see the sunshine bounce off her auburn ponytail. The bright light also revealed faint tear trails on her cheeks. Her lashes were damp and, for the first time, he realized she had freckles on her nose.

Those light freckles made her seem younger, and she looked achingly vulnerable sitting all alone at the big table in the empty restaurant.

"Jenna?" he asked gently, his guilt magnified by her obvious distress. Had he caused this?

She glanced up, seemingly startled by his voice. Anxiety flicked through her green eyes and she grabbed a crumpled tissue, dabbing at her cheeks.

"What do you want?" she asked in a hoarse voice.

"What's wrong?"

"Nothing."

"You're upset."

"I'm fine."

"You're crying."

"Go away."

"Come on, Jenna. What's going on?" He felt like the world's biggest heel. Was it even worse than he thought? Did she know about his contract with Brandon?

"Please just go away," she said, turning her attention to the drawing in front of her. It depicted the restaurant in front of her, but with blond wood paneling, huge windows, and plenty of potted plants.

"Looks nice," he said, tilting his head to a better angle.

"Right." Her answer was chopped and terse. She was definitely still mad at him.

If she knew about his contract with Brandon, he was toast. If she was only upset because he'd walked away from their kiss, at least he had a fighting chance.

"You're getting rid of the bar?" he asked, pointing to her drawing, trying to engage her in casual conversation while he figured out what was going on.

She shrugged without meeting his gaze, fidgeting with her pencil.

"The skylights are nice."

She still didn't answer.

He slipped into the chair beside her. Forget wheedling his way in with inconsequential conversation. He might as well get right to it.

"Are you still mad at me?" he asked, steeling himself as he waited to find out how much she knew, prepared to beg her forgiveness right here and now.

He was met with silence again.

All right. He was going to assume walking away

from the kiss was the problem. Might as well be an optimist as long as possible.

"Because I can explain," he said. "In fact, I've been looking—"

"This isn't about you, Tyler." Her voice was cold and distant as she snapped her pencil down on the table. "You're not interested in me? Fine. No problem. Life does go on."

Fine? No problem? Well, it was sure a big problem to him. He didn't want life to go on. Not hers or his until they took care of this.

"If you'll just let me—"

"Nothing wrong with your ego, is there?" She finally looked at him. The flashing anger in her green eyes competed with the sunlight streaming in through the window.

"I'm just trying to—"

"What part of 'not about you' are you struggling with?"

"I just thought..." He scrutinized her expression, turning silent as her words penetrated.

She was serious.

It wasn't him.

It was *good* that she wasn't upset with him.

No, wait a minute, it was bad. If he hadn't upset her, then it could be something truly serious. Unless it was Brandon. Maybe Brandon had broken things off.

"Then what is wrong?" He reached up to brush

back a wisp of hair that had escaped from her ponytail, grasping at the flimsy excuse to touch her.

"I just want to be alone. Is that too much to ask?"

"How can I leave you alone?" There was no way he was walking away from a woman in distress. Especially this woman.

He stroked her damp cheek with the pad of his thumb. "Please let me help."

She drew away from his touch. "*You* want to help *me?*"

"Right."

"Forgive me for being skeptical about your intentions." Her laugh was hollow.

"I'm so sorry if I hurt you."

She didn't answer.

"Please believe that I care about you, Jenna."

"You don't know me, Tyler."

Well, that was sure true enough. "Then let me know you. I want to know you."

"Bare my emotions to you?" she snapped, then glanced around the empty room and lowered her voice. "My body wasn't enough? You want my soul before you walk away this time?"

"I can explain."

"Sure, you can."

"I wouldn't walk away."

"You've done it twice."

"Not by choice." Maybe he should just tell her what happened.

No. He needed to show her. He needed to prove beyond a shadow of a doubt that he had a legitimate reason for walking away.

"Really?" she asked. "It seems to me that both times *I* made a choice to stay. I was the one making a fool—"

"There was a reason. Come to my room with me."

She gave him a look that clearly questioned his sanity.

"I swear I won't touch you." He held up both hands. "There's something I need to show you."

"I've got work to do."

"Just give me a chance to prove I'm not a jerk."

"I did." She glared.

"And I blew it." He closed his eyes for a split second.

"Twice," she said.

He paused, regrouping. "There's a logical explanation."

"Can't wait to see what that is."

He looked deep into her sea green eyes, not about to let that opening pass. "It's in my room. Let me show you."

"Tyler."

"You're a very special woman, and I don't want you to think badly of me."

Her eyes shuttered closed for a second. "Tyler, I can't—"

"Please," he implored, shocked by how much he needed to clear the air.

"This is way too complicated," she said. "On top of everything else, I don't have time to—"

"Half an hour," he pressed. "That's all I ask. And, afterward, if you want me to walk out of your life, I will."

"Why should I trust you?"

He paused for a minute, then responded honestly. "You shouldn't."

Her expression softened. "Finally, we agree on something."

"We agree on a lot of things."

"Such as?"

"The bordello look." He offered her a coaxing smile. "I had fun that night, Jenna."

She sighed in apparent exasperation, but he could tell she was weakening.

"Half an hour," he repeated. "I promise."

"Fine," she nodded.

"Yeah?" Relief coursed through him.

She glanced at her watch. "You're on the clock."

WHAT WAS SHE DOING HERE? Jenna warily stepped over the threshold into Tyler's suite. She shouldn't even give him the time of day.

She was crazy to see him alone after his behavior... After her reaction... Not that she was afraid she'd weaken or anything.

It was just... Well, his apparent sincerity had got to her. She was used to Brandon's slick, sophisticated brand of persuasion. She hadn't had time to build up a defense against Tyler's apparent honesty.

But, this was it, she promised herself. His "logical" explanation was sure to reveal his true nature. After that, she'd be free of him for good. No more lingering daydreams or secret longings for what might have been.

He'd asked for half an hour? She'd give him ten minutes. Then she was out of here.

She glanced around the big room.

"Why is it that a security guard..." She gestured to the mahogany table set for ten with imported china and crystal, and the two living room groupings, one of which flanked a stone fireplace. Huge bunches of fresh flowers perfumed the air.

She loved fresh flowers.

"Well...Henry's asked me to work some extra shifts." Tyler seemed amazingly at home in the opulent surroundings.

"You're telling me that for extra shifts, Henry gave you the best suite in the hotel?" Was there more to Tyler than met the eye?

"Second best." Tyler smiled. "You should see the Roosevelt Suite," he said. "Now that's luxury."

His blue eyes sparkled. "This one just happened to be available," he said easily. "The bankers' convention is taking up most of the regular rooms. But, believe me, if a paying guest shows up, lowly ol' me is kicked right out of here."

Jenna cracked a half smile. Despite his predisposition for revving her up to a hundred and then pulling the emergency brake, she couldn't help but appreciate his unpretentious mannerisms.

She found herself hoping that his logical explanation was indeed logical. Then at least she'd know it wasn't her hopeless kissing technique that had turned him off. And maybe there'd be hope for her and somebody someday.

"Have a seat," he invited softly, gesturing to one of the Dresden blue sofas.

Jenna lowered herself onto the cushion at one end, pressing herself against the padded arm, suddenly apprehensive. If he made a move on her, she was going to have to run for it. She'd have to run far and fast before his easy charm and his midnight eyes undid her resolve.

To her relief, he didn't take the space next to her. Instead, he crossed the room to open the wide wooden doors on the entertainment center. He popped a tape into the VCR.

"What are you—"

"Just watch," he said, moving so that he was standing behind her and slightly to her left, pointing the remote control at the screen.

He was going to show her home movies in order to explain his behavior?

Of what? His wife? His kids? His dog?

How would that justify anything? Unless Mrs. Carter was a crazy woman locked up in the attic of the gothic family home. Or maybe she was ill, confined to a hospital for years on end, and Tyler was torn between his duty and his desire.

No. That was silly. Mrs. Carter was probably a perfectly nice woman, living in... Maybe that was it. Maybe she lived far away, and Tyler was lonely.

Lonely, but unable to bring himself to cheat. Admirable. Sort of.

Jenna didn't want to see home movies of Mrs. Carter. She didn't want to lust after a married man.

The screen lit up, drawing her gaze. The hotel spa came into view. It was empty. No Mrs. Carter so far.

Jenna stilled for a moment, perched on the edge of the couch.

The picture wasn't perfect, black-and-white and a little bit grainy. Then suddenly, *she* came into view.

Jenna slumped back in astonishment, feeling the blood drain from her face as she watched herself walk from the tearoom to the whirlpool. On screen, she gazed wordlessly into the depths of the swirling water.

Thank goodness Tyler couldn't tell what she'd been thinking as she dipped her foot into the water, then sat down, then shimmied her dress up out of the way.

The sensations of cool tile and warm water rushed back to her.

She stared in silence at her wide eyes and parted lips—remembering, feeling. For a second she was positive every sensual thought entering her mind was written there on her face for the world to see.

"Who?" she squeaked.

"Nobody." Tyler put a comforting hand on her shoulder. "Nobody but me has seen it."

Jenna nodded, half-relieved, half-mortified, as she watched herself walk across the spa to the secluded pool. Thank goodness nobody else had seen it.

But Tyler had seen it. Had he known? Could he tell? Had he figured out what she was imagining for those few moments she'd been alone?

On the screen, she disappeared in the little alcove. Then her dress flopped over the rattan and vine divider. So, he definitely knew she'd been naked back there.

His fingers convulsed against her shoulder, sending a pulse of desire through her chest.

The dress suddenly disappeared from the divider, and she remembered her mad scramble to put it back on. And her panties. Oh, good grief, she'd turfed her panties in the spa.

When Tyler appeared on camera, the memories of the night forced the breath from her lungs. She stared at the television screen as he pulled her into his arms.

Even in black-and-white, their kisses seemed to set the room on fire.

She remembered the smell of his skin, the sound of his breathing, the taste of his kisses and the rough texture of his hands. Her palms grew damp, and she felt sweat gathering between her breasts as she watched him pull her dress up, further, out of the way of his questing hands.

Then, on the screen, Tyler suddenly froze. He stared straight into the camera. His eyes widened in horror and he quickly yanked her dress down.

She instantly had her answer.

That's why he'd stopped. It was in his expression, plastered in front of her, leaving no doubt whatsoever. He'd seen the camera, and tried to extricate her from the situation.

She should have thanked him. Instead, she watched her reaction and wanted to yell at her image to quit being such a shrew. He was trying to save her, and she'd torn a strip off him, telling him she never wanted to see him again.

As the spa door clicked shut behind her image, she let eyelids drift shut in embarrassment and, heaven help her, arousal. She wanted to apologize to him right now, but she didn't think she could speak. Seeing herself in Tyler's arms, under his hands, under his lips, responding with passion and abandon to his kisses, had been intensely arousing.

Her chest was tight, her extremities tingling, and

her lips felt deprived. If she said or did anything right now, it would be to throw herself into his arms and beg him to finish what they'd started two days ago.

The empty spa stared back at her for a long minute. Jenna could feel her heart beating, her lungs laboring, lips tingling.

Tyler was silent beside her, his hand had dropped away from her shoulder, but she could feel him watching. His sleeve rustled against his shirt in the silent room, and he drew in a deep breath.

Something clicked, and the tape started to rewind.

It clicked again and there he was, walking into the spa in instant replay.

Jenna felt herself lean forward in anticipation. It was embarrassing, but she couldn't drag her gaze away from their images.

Tyler moved quietly behind the couch, rounding the end. Then he settled onto the cushion beside her.

She couldn't bring herself to acknowledge him. This was hands down the most intimate and erotic experience of her life, and she was half-scared, half-thrilled by it.

On screen, Tyler brushed back her hair. Sitting beside her, the real Tyler followed suit.

She tensed and had to bite back a moan.

On screen, he kissed her mouth.

The real Tyler kissed her temple, whispering meaningless words in her ear.

She could feel the moist heat of his lips on her skin, and she could see him there on the screen.

On he went, following the script, letting her watch. When he slowly pulled down the neckline of her real dress, scraping it over her nipples just like in their private movie, she couldn't hold back her moan.

When he bent to kiss her breast, she gasped his name. Then, when his on-screen hands fisted in the fabric, he pulled her to her feet in the hotel room.

He pinned her with a smoky blue stare and resolutely bent to kiss her mouth.

Sensations rocketed through her as his tongue parried and thrust. His hands went to work on her dress, pulling it up out of the way.

She was wearing panties this time, and he toyed with the edge of the elastic, thumbs slipping beneath, tracing a line across her inner thigh. Brushing, touching, arousing.

"I never would have stopped," he breathed in her ear between kisses. "Not in a million years."

She groaned, wriggling against his hand. She started working on the buttons of his shirt, desperate to feel his skin. She wanted to taste him, breathe him in, catapult blindly into sensations she'd never experienced before.

"But I had to get the tape." He nipped at her earlobe, his tongue teasing every sensitive spot on her neck. "I couldn't take the chance that somebody..."

"Why didn't you tell me sooner?" she gasped.

She'd been suffering for two whole days. She could have had this. She could have had him. He could have relieved the intense ache grasping at her body.

"I've been looking for you all over the place." He cupped her chin. "All *over* the place." Then he captured her in an open-mouthed kiss that blasted sensation all the way to her toes.

"You've found me now," she breathed. Had he ever.

He shrugged out of his shirt, and swiftly peeled off her dress, stepping back, looking his fill.

"I liked you better without underwear," he said.

"I can fix that."

"Good."

"But first..." She reached for the button on his pants. "You're lagging behind."

"Can't have that." He started to help her with the button, and soon they were both naked.

Jenna gazed at his gorgeous body. Then she slowly smiled. He was better than any old whirlpool. She reached out a trembling hand and brushed his belly with the back of her knuckles.

He sucked in a breath.

He grasped her wrist, then drew her forward, lifting her into his arms, kissing her mouth as he headed for the bedroom, dousing the lights, slipping her through the doorway.

There, he laid her back on the king-size bed, following her down, settling between her legs, kissing, nuzzling, teasing. "Look," he whispered.

She opened her eyes and followed the direction of his nod. There they were, back-lit by the distant glow of the sunset, in life-size glory, reflected in the mirrored closet doors.

He moved, and she watched, transfixed. She felt his slick skin rub against her own. She heard his breathing echoing in her ears, and felt the rhythm of his heart against her rib cage.

She met his eyes in the mirror and thought she should be embarrassed. But she wasn't.

He cupped one hand under her bottom, bending her knees, drawing her to him.

"I sure hope you don't have to be anywhere for a long, long time," he whispered.

7

"IT FEELS LIKE I waited forever," said Tyler, letting his fingertip trail along Jenna's bare stomach, enjoying the warmth of her skin all over again. They were cuddled, spoon fashion, under the big comforter on his bed. The curtains were open, and a million stars lit up the sky above the black lake.

"I've waited my whole life," she whispered back.

"Are you saying I'm the best you ever had?" He joked, kissing the back of her neck, loving the taste of her skin, the tickle of the fine hairs at her nape, inhaling her all over again.

"By a mile."

Tyler's arms flexed around her. He couldn't help the surge of male pride that filled him. But, it was followed immediately by an attack of jealousy. Brandon had been in her life once, and probably would be again.

But, he wasn't going to think about Brandon right now. Or the consequences of what he'd just done. Tomorrow was soon enough for recrimination and restitution.

For tonight, he was only going to think about Jenna. And about how he could keep her smiling.

"What upset you in the restaurant?" he asked, wanting nothing more than for her life to be perfect.

Her slender shoulders shrugged against his chest.

"Was it me?" he asked.

She'd denied it earlier, but she might have been lying.

After a long pause, she whispered, "It was me. My stupidity. My mistake."

"What happened?" He had a hard time believing she'd done anything stupid. Him. Now he was a walking poster boy for dumb mistakes.

Jenna nodded, drawing a shuddering breath and plucking at the comforter. "Henry didn't like my redecorating sketches. He turned them down."

"He fired you?" Tyler drew back. He couldn't believe it. The sketch he'd seen in the restaurant was terrific. Jenna was obviously very talented. He couldn't imagine how Henry could have failed to see it.

He had to fight an urge to reach for the phone, invoke the dreaded family name and demand that Henry tell him what the hell was going on.

Jenna shook her head. "I have one more chance."

Tyler breathed a sigh of relief. Thank goodness he didn't have to compromise his independence and alienate Henry. It would be nice to end the evening with at least one principle intact.

Jenna shifted, tightening against him. "But I'm *so* scared."

"Don't be scared." He pushed his own problems to the back of his mind and gathered her close. "You'll do great."

"I didn't do so great last time."

"Fluke. You're brilliant."

"And, that assessment is based on...what?" There was a smile in her voice. One that he wanted to keep there.

"You have excellent taste in men. I'm convinced that means you have excellent taste in everything else."

She shifted onto her back, looking up at him in the moonlight. "What an ego."

"Seriously." He stroked his thumb across her bottom lip. It was bright pink and slightly swollen. The sight turned him on.

He squelched the urge to lean down and kiss her. "People are good at the things they love. It's when their family...

"I mean, when other people push them into something they don't like, that they fail. You love decorating, right?"

"I do." She nodded. "Always have."

"That's why you'll succeed."

Jenna stared up at him in silence for a few moments. Man, oh man, did he want to kiss her again. To drag her close and make love to her all over again.

He settled for brushing the stray hairs off her forehead. They glinted in the moonlight beneath his fingers.

"That sounded personal."

"Personal?"

"Is somebody trying to push you into something?" she asked.

Tyler stilled, afraid of revealing too much, desperate to let her get closer.

"Your family?" she pressed.

He nodded, settling on his elbow, gazing into the depths of her eyes. Green, he knew, but he hadn't realized they had little gold flecks as well.

"Your father?" she asked.

"You're smart," he affirmed.

She smiled. "Did he want you to grow up to be a doctor? A lawyer? An accountant?"

"He wanted me to join the family firm." Tyler was treading on dangerous ground, but he wanted her to know at least a little bit about the real him.

"Which is?"

He hesitated. "Importing and exporting mostly." On a scale that would boggle many people's minds.

Jenna's eyebrows shot up, and she tilted her head. "Are they involved in organized crime?"

Tyler barked out a laugh. "No. They're not involved in organized crime."

"Oh. I always thought the mysterious 'importing

and exporting' tag was a euphemism for criminal activity. Like drugs or gunrunning."

"No drugs. No guns." Pharmaceuticals, sure. But everything was legal.

"What kinds of things do they import?"

"Refrigerators and microwave ovens." Technically true. Tyler was pretty sure there was an appliance division buried somewhere under the shipping lines and holding companies.

"So, why didn't you make your dad happy and join up as a junior executive?"

"Why aren't you farming in Minnesota?"

"Minnesota farmhouses are singularly plain structures. I'd wither away and die."

"Refrigerators and microwave ovens are singularly boring. I'd wither away and die."

"So, import something different." She rolled onto her side, imitating his posture, her little elbow making a dent in the plump pillow. "Import something exciting."

"And succeed on my father's shoulders?"

"Aha!" She smiled.

"What, aha?"

"I've discovered your secret. *You* have an independent streak."

"Nothing wrong with that. When I make my fortune, it's going to be *my* fortune. Nobody is going to tell me how to earn it or spend it."

"I didn't think security guards made fortunes."

"I'm not just a security guard. I have my own...security business."

"Make much money?"

"Not lately."

"Me neither. Well, unless I can woo Henry with some new ideas."

"You will."

"You're pretty confident for a guy who doesn't know anything about me."

"I know everything about you." He settled closer, pulling her into his arms again, running his hands along her bare back. "Everything that counts, anyway."

She tipped her head back to look into his eyes. "Are you suggesting my body is more important than my mind?"

"No. Of course not." He kissed his way down her neck. "Please, tell me more about your mind."

She laughed.

He drew back, smoothing her hair. "I'm serious. Now that you know my secret, tell me about you. Something important. Something nobody else knows."

"There aren't many things in my life that nobody knows."

"Your hopes. Your dreams. What made you want to become a decorator in the first place?"

She paused, and got a faraway look in her eyes. "I've always wanted to make things beautiful. People don't understand. Even if you don't notice it, beautiful surroundings have an incredible effect on your psyche."

"Can't argue with that," said Tyler. "You're beautiful. And you are having one incredible effect on my psyche."

"I'm serious."

"So am I. But lets keep talking about decorating." He brushed the freckles on her nose with his index finger. "For now."

"When I was five years old..." She leaned back on the white pillowcase, staring into the star scattered night. "I don't usually tell people about this, you know. It could compromise my professional integrity."

"Your secret is safe with me," he whispered.

"My secrets better be safe with you. You've got me naked on video tape."

"And I didn't sell it to a tabloid. So you know that I'm perfectly trustworthy. Go on. Give."

"Okay. When I was five years old, I made curtains for our kitchen window."

"That doesn't sound so bad."

"Ugliest little things in the world." She laughed softly. "I found an old sheet in the rag bin and cut it up with my kindergarten scissors. Used a needle and thread for part of it, but then I got lazy and switched to Scotch tape."

"How did they look?" he asked.

"Horrible. The sheet was worn white and thread-bare in the middle, the edges were still lime green. I swear my mom was about to rip them down, but dad stopped her."

"Nice man."

"He was. Holidays came and went. Friends and relatives visited. And the silly things hung there like an eyesore for three whole years."

"That's sweet. What happened to them?"

"Steven—or was it Mitch?—lit them on fire."

"On purpose?"

"No." She chuckled and shook her head. "Though they probably deserved it. But we had a lot of power failures. They were lighting the oil lamp."

"Anybody hurt?"

"No. Mom put it out pretty fast."

"So lighting the tablecloth in the restaurant was just a long-standing family tradition."

"Must have been."

"I was *so* attracted to you that night," he couldn't help remembering out loud.

She smiled and looked back up at him. "In a lady-of-the-evening sort of way?"

He chuckled and kissed the tip of her shoulder. "In a woman-I-can't-keep-my-hands-off sort of way. So, who are Steven and Mitch?" He rushed into a new question before she could think to ask why he'd backed off the first night.

Damn, he did *not* want to be investigating her right now.

"My brothers," she answered.

"Older than you? Armed? Lurking anywhere in the greater Seattle area?" He could feel himself slipping further and further into trouble here.

Jenna laughed. "Younger. All of them. Still in Minnesota."

"So, I'm safe." Except for Brandon. But Brandon was far away in Boston.

"I'd say so." She gave an exaggerated sigh. "Steven, Mitch and Randy. The messy little horde. The bane of my curtain-making, flower-picking, picture-hanging existence."

"They were Bohemians?"

"They were Bohemians, and my mother was the consummate minimalist. Plain, flat, beige and boring. Did I tell you we lived on a wheat farm?"

He shook his head. "Just that it was Minnesota."

"Muddy. Muddy in the spring, muddy in the fall. Bohemian boys tromping mud into the flat, beige kitchen. And me filling jelly jars with flowers and making curtains out of old sheets. Pathetic, isn't it?"

"It's admirable. Even back then you wanted to make things beautiful."

Jenna curled her legs and sat up against the headboard. "And, I'm still trying to make things beautiful for people who don't want me to do it."

"Henry will come around," said Tyler.

"Only if I come up with some better ideas."

"You will."

"Maybe."

Tyler sat up beside her. "Tell me about Boston."

"What do you want to know?"

"What did you do there?"

"I went to school."

"Who were your friends?"

"Candice."

"What about men?"

"You fishing for another compliment?"

"Huh?"

She walked her fingertips along his bare chest. "I already told you you're the best I've ever had."

Evasive maneuver. Just like in the restaurant. The woman obviously had something to hide.

Like you don't? a little voice pointed out.

"Hungry?" she asked. "'Cause I'm getting really hungry here."

"Sure." He backed off. He had a gorgeous, naked woman in his bed. Why the hell would he want to broach the subject of Boston and Brandon anyway?

"What do you want?" he asked. "We could call room service. Or there are some snacks in the bar."

"What's in the bar?" She sat up straighter.

Tyler shifted out of bed and padded into the living room. "Looks like we've got a complete meal," he called back. "Pretzels, champagne and chocolate-covered almonds."

"I keep trying to tell Candice that chocolate-covered almonds are a food group."

"Grapes qualify as a fruit." He held up the champagne bottle on his way back to the bedroom. "Everything we need. Celebratory *and* nutritious."

"What are we celebrating?"

"Let me see..." He paused in the doorway. Man, she looked good in his bed.

"Us," he answered, setting the glasses down on the bedside table and popping the cork. He poured some of the effervescent champagne into each one.

Jenna crossed her legs and wrapped the quilt around herself, accepting one of the glasses.

"You know," she said. "For a one-night stand, this doesn't feel at all tacky."

"What one-night stand?" He sat down next to her, stretching his legs back under the covers. "It took me four whole days just to get you here."

"Poor baby," she grinned.

"Four excruciating days of foreplay and frustration."

"Impatient, are you?"

"As a matter of fact, I'm normally a very patient man."

"I noticed." A slight blush rose on her cheeks. "Thanks." She dipped her head to sip the champagne.

"That wasn't patience," Tyler corrected. "That was savoring the moment."

He waited to meet her eyes, and then stared into them for a silent heartbeat. "And I want to savor it all over again."

"Now?"

"For starters." He held up his glass. "To savoring us, Jenna."

A hint of uncertainty flashed through her expression as she clinked her glass against his. Tyler's chest tightened. Some how, some way, he had to make her see Brandon was all wrong.

"WHERE WERE YOU last night?" asked Candice as she crossed the threshold into Jenna's hotel suite.

"Sorry." Jenna stepped back, letting the door swing shut automatically behind the crisply outfitted Candice.

It was eight in the morning. Jenna had left Tyler's suite around five. Even then, she'd been reluctant to say goodbye. They'd lingered beside the door, him peppering her with random kisses, her insisting he didn't need to escort her down two floors.

After a couple scant hours of sleep, she was tired and tender, but energized at the same time. Making love with Tyler was beyond anything she'd ever imagined. He was earthy and honest, attentive, and so full of life.

"The last time was 2:00 a.m." Candice gave her a significant look as she waltzed across the cream-colored carpet to the fresh tray of coffee on the bar.

"I was with *him*," Jenna admitted. No point in keeping it a secret from Candice. Not that she even wanted to.

Candice had been her stalwart confidante through the rough Brandon years. She deserved to share in the good stuff, too. And Tyler was definitely the good stuff.

"Him who?" Candice poured herself a cup of black coffee.

"The guy who walked away." Jenna retrieved her own full cup from where she'd set it on a side table.

"Tyler?" Candice turned, cup poised.

"Right."

"You were with Tyler until two in the morning?"

"He didn't walk away this time." Jenna couldn't help the secretive grin that formed on her face.

"Holy cow." Candice dropped her purse and sank into a plush armchair, looking astonished.

"You got that right," said Jenna.

Candice blinked up at her. "I take it he made it past the three minute mark."

"I think we made it past the three hour mark."

"You sure you're ready for this?"

"For what? Wild, crazy, mind-blowing sex?"

"Wow." Candice crossed her legs and adjusted her short skirt. "And to think I was excited to tell you that the hospital lobby is finished."

"Well, that's great, too." Jenna took the opposite chair.

Candice sipped her coffee. A sly grin formed on her face. "Yeah. But my news has suddenly been put into glaring perspective."

"I'm afraid I have some bad news on the company front," said Jenna, refusing to let herself put it off any longer. By rights, she should have called Candice last night.

"Well, that seems only fair," said Candice. "To balance things off, I mean." She paused, looking intently at Jenna. "Tyler all night long. Wow."

Wow, was right. Last night had been one wow moment after another. Jenna took a healthy swallow of coffee, letting the welcome shot of caffeine invade her system.

Candice watched her from across the room. "I take it you're completely over Brandon."

"Brandon who?"

"That's the spirit." Candice tipped her head back and laughed. "It's a brave new world, babe. You've finally experienced great sex, and there's not a stray P.I. in sight."

"Isn't it terrific?" Jenna was free. Completely and totally free. Her years with Brandon might never have even happened.

"It's terrific, all right." Candice set her cup down on the oak end table. "Now instead of sitting there after-glowing and making me all jealous, why don't you hit me with your bad news?"

"Hmm. Right." Jenna's euphoric bubble burst. "I'm afraid this isn't just *my* bad news," she warned.

"No?"

"Henry didn't like the sketches."

Candice's smile disappeared, a disappointed grimace taking its place. "Did he fire us?"

"We have one more chance. Listen, I'm sorry I didn't run the final sketches past you before I showed them to Henry—"

Candice shook her head. "We can't micromanage each other, remember?"

"But, you took such a chance on me."

"You're in it with me."

"It's mostly your money."

"We've had this argument before." Candice made a dismissive motion with one hand. "I won, you lost. We're partners."

"But—"

"Show me the sketches, and tell me what he said." She pushed up the sleeves on her sweater. "Let's figure out what we have to do to fix this."

Right. The pragmatic approach. That's what Jenna loved about Candice.

She crossed to the desk and pulled out her portfolio. "I started something new yesterday before...well, before I met up with Tyler again."

She laid the pile of sketches down in front of Candice, tightening the belt on her robe.

"What did he say?" asked Candice.

"Tyler?"

"No." Candice grinned. "Him later. Henry now. What did Henry say?"

"His biggest problem," said Jenna, turning her attention to the sketches. "Was that they weren't innovative enough. He said money is no object. And, you know, Candice, I think he means it."

"As in..."

"As in, the board's prepared to spend millions."

"Millions?" Candice's eyes went wide.

"He's not sure we can think big enough."

"We can think plenty big."

"Maybe. But you know who we need to talk to about this?"

"Who?"

"Derek."

"Derek?" Candice shook her head. "He doesn't know a thing about decorating."

"Maybe not. But he had the authority to hire us."

Candice harrumphed. "I don't want anything to do with that egomaniac."

"Derek is an egomaniac?" Jenna sure hadn't noticed that about him.

"You couldn't tell? Gads, he reminds me of my dad and my brothers. He's the king of the world, and we are but the little people sent to populate his playground."

"I didn't get—"

"Did you see his suit? His shoes? His car? Talk about flaunting your wealth."

"I thought he was pretty understated. For a guy who can give out million dollar contracts in less than thirty minutes."

Candice shook her head, laughing hollowly. "Anybody who knows what they're looking for can spot his money from five hundred yards. It's like a game to them. I am *so* glad I've stayed away from my family's business and their friends and their lifestyle."

"Rich or not, Derek might be able to help us," said Jenna, anxious to make sure they succeeded this time. Losing a contract at the conceptual designs stage would be worse than never having a chance at it in the first place.

They had to make this work.

"Then you meet with him," said Candice, flipping through the sketches.

"We both go," said Jenna with determination. "We can't fool around here, Candice. We're in too deep. We need to make this work, and I need you there with me."

"Fine," Candice sighed, coming to the end of the sketch pile. "I guess I can put up with the man for an hour or so. It's not like he even looks at me."

Jenna stared at the top of her friend's head. Candice never cared if men noticed her or not. Quite frankly, the attention she usually garnered from the opposite sex annoyed her more than it flattered her.

But, for some reason, she cared about Derek's attention. Jenna smiled as she remembered the way Candice had defended his "brawny" looks in the lobby the other day.

The more Jenna thought about it, the more she could picture sparks flying between Derek and Candice. Maybe...

"These are good, Jenna." Candice patted the pile of sketches. "You might not have spent enough of their millions with these ideas, but they give us a starting point."

"Henry didn't like them," Jenna pointed out.

Candice waved a hand in the air. "I didn't say we wouldn't change them. Just that they were a starting point. I still think Scandinavian is the right direction. Heaven knows we should get rid of the dark, old money oppression around here."

Jenna pulled out the business card Derek had given her that first day. "I'm making an appointment with Derek for tomorrow."

"Speaking of dark, oppressive old money..."

"Give the guy a chance." Jenna began dialing Derek's cell phone number.

8

TYLER STARED at his progress report to Brandon on the hotel room computer. He'd reported on Jenna's contract at the hotel. The fact that she was staying at the hotel. Her dinner at the Lighthouse restaurant with an unknown man. Their visit to Henry's office.

He decided their kiss in the office wasn't significant. Dinner with a strange man was probably enough to make Brandon question the wisdom of his engagement. Besides, if Tyler had been the P.I. out in the hallway, instead of the unnamed man in Henry's office, he wouldn't have known about the kiss anyway.

He did, however report on their kiss in the spa, making it sound as though the whole thing happened while the spa was open. Technically, he hadn't lied at all in the report. And he was definitely giving Brandon the image of a fiancée with an outside love interest. Hopefully, it would cause Brandon to break up with her.

Although, if he was honest with himself, what Tyler really wanted was for Jenna to break up with

Brandon. He wanted her to decide that wealth wasn't worth sacrificing for.

He plunked away at the computer keys, detailing what he knew, or what he *should* know as a P.I., carefully wording the rest of the progress report.

Jenna was an intelligent, hardworking, upstanding woman. He had every confidence that she'd decide for herself soon enough what was important in life. Tyler was positive she wouldn't choose Brandon. But there was no harm in helping out a little.

When he was finished, he hit the print key.

He set the clean copy on the fax machine and punched in Brandon's office number.

Then he went looking for Jenna.

HE FOUND HER with Candice in one of the hotel lounges. It was closed until noon, and they were alone on a small, wrought-iron balcony that overlooked the main lobby.

Their backs were to him, and they both had sketch pads on their knees. The teapot, empty cups and scattered papers attested to the fact that they'd been working there for a long time.

"Hi," he breathed, drawing close to Jenna's chair. He longed to reach out and touch her, but he wasn't sure what she'd told Candice about their relationship.

Jenna looked up.

"Hi, Tyler." She smiled and a funny, squeezing sensation gripped his chest. Then, to his immense satisfaction, she reached for his hand and brushed a light kiss across his knuckles.

Oh, well, if that was the case...

He leaned down and planted a kiss on her mouth. She responded, tasting of blueberry tea. Either Candice was a very willing accomplice in deceiving Brandon, or Jenna was already having second thoughts about the engagement. Either one worked for Tyler at the moment, since it meant he could touch Jenna.

"This is my partner, Candice Hammond," said Jenna, reminding Tyler that he wasn't supposed to know Candice yet.

"Nice to meet you, Candice." He straightened, but kept one hand on the back of Jenna's hair. He'd only seen Candice once, from a distance, so he hadn't put her name and her looks together. But now recognition twigged as he held out his hand.

She was a Hammond. One of *the* Hammonds. The family look was unmistakable. And her father and brothers were direct competitors of the Reeves-DuCarter electronics division. Derek's baby.

Why hadn't Derek mentioned this?

He folded himself into the little ice-cream parlor style chair next to Jenna, telling himself that Candice wouldn't find out anything about his family ties. It wasn't like he was active in Reeves-DuCarter. And he'd never met her father and brother in person. He'd only seen them in pictures. And, of course, he knew them by reputation.

"How's it going?" He gazed at the sketch in front of Jenna, stroking her hair again, enjoying the sense of serenity that drifted over him now that he was with her.

"We're sticking with Scandinavian." She pointed to a pile of sketches with her pencil. "Take a look at the ones for the restaurant."

Tyler picked up the papers and leafed through them. She'd boldly eliminated the heavy beams, replacing them with square, white pillars. The leather and mahogany bar was still gone from the middle of the room, and windows and skylights had taken over the walls and ceilings.

She'd even sketched in a waiter in a designer uniform instead of a tux.

"I don't know," he teased. "I'll miss the bordello look."

She shot him a worried glance.

"Joking." He shook his head. This was miles above the existing decor. "I'm sorry. I love your ideas. I love them all."

"Really?" Her posture relaxed. "I'm getting really nervous."

"It's going great," Candice put in. "But, the stakes are pretty high."

"How so?" Tyler asked.

"If we succeed," said Candice, "it can catapult us to a whole new professional level. It's by far the biggest contract we've ever undertaken."

"The biggest?" asked Tyler.

"Easily," said Candice.

"And Henry knew this when he hired you?"

Henry was a terrific hotel manager but, along with Tyler's father—and Candice's father, too for that matter—he was a charter member of the Old Boys Club. It wasn't like him to take a chance on an unproven firm.

Unless Candice's father had pulled some strings to get them the job. Which made no sense whatsoever. A Hammond would never ask a favor of a Reeves-DuCarter. And a Reeves-DuCarter would never grant it.

"We didn't lie," said Jenna.

"I never thought you did," Tyler hastily said.

"So, Tyler." Candice drew a long sweeping line across the top of her page, eyeing up the lobby and then looking back down at the paper. "Tell me about your intentions towards Jenna."

"Candice," Jenna gasped.

Quite frankly, Tyler's intentions were to undermine Jenna's relationship with her fiancé and keep her in his bed just as long as he could get away with it.

"Strictly dishonorable." His tone made a joke of the word, but deep down inside he knew that it was true. And the guilt he'd been repressing since yesterday was beginning to show itself. He had some tough de-

cisions to make about who he was working for and
how much he was telling Jenna.

"*Good,*" said Candice. "That's exactly what she
needs in her life right now. Help her put things in
perspective."

"Candice," Jenna warned in an undertone, obviously worried her friend would elaborate.

"It's the truth," said Candice, without looking up.

Tyler watched Candice's expression with interest.
He assumed Candice preferred him to Brandon. Perfect. Candice would be a welcome ally.

"Glad I have your blessing," he said heartily, pretending to be oblivious to the undercurrents between
the two women.

"I'm going for more tea." Candice stood up and
lifted the pot. "You want anything?" she asked Tyler.

He jumped up from his chair. "I can go." With the
lounge closed, there were no waiters on the floor.

Candice shook her head. "I need to stretch my legs
anyway. I can bring you something back."

He shook his head. "I'm good."

"Keep working," she said to Jenna as she turned to
leave.

Tyler sat back down and captured Jenna's left
hand. Her right one was busy on the sketch pad draft-
ing out the lobby.

He kissed her knuckles. "I miss you."

"Me, too."

"When can we get together and do something dishonorable?"

She smiled without looking up. "I've got a ton of things to do in the next couple of days."

"Oh." He tried not to let his disappointment show. "It would have to be quick."

"Quick and dishonorable?" His interest perked up.

She glanced at him for a split second and her sensual expression sizzled right through him. "Yeah."

"Works for me." He sat back in the chair, stroking his thumb across her knuckles, gazing at the people milling around the busy lobby, while she continued working. "You just name the time and place."

"Anywhere without security cameras."

"I thought you liked being in the movies." And, quite frankly, he loved that she liked it.

She didn't say anything, and she didn't look up.

"Jenna?"

She scribbled frantically.

"Are you embarrassed?"

She still didn't answer, just kept right on drawing.

"Sweetheart? Hey?" He tipped his head so that he could see her face.

She was blushing.

"Anything you want is okay with me." He slipped off the chair and crouched in front of her. "There aren't any rules of etiquette. You're allowed to get turned on by movies or mirrors or leather or lace."

Her gaze rose, green eyes starting to smolder.

"Or by me telling you how gorgeous you are, and how I can't wait until you've finished working today so that you can get naked and climb into my bed."

She kept staring at him, her chest rising and falling as her breathing grew deeper.

He was onto something here. He let his voice drop. "Where I'll kiss every inch of your naked body…"

She stared at him, transfixed, eyes widening, lips softening.

"Until you moan my name and wrap your legs around my waist…" He trailed his fingers up the inside of her thigh.

Her grip tightened on the arm of the chair.

"Just as long as it's me, Jenna," he whispered. "That's my only stipulation." As he said the words, he realized how frighteningly true they'd become. "It has to be with me."

She gasped in a breath and nodded.

Tyler smiled.

"Got the tea here," Candice sang out.

THERE WAS AN honesty about Tyler. It wasn't just the way he made love. It was everything he said and did.

He was down to earth, unpretentious. And, after trying so hard to please Brandon for all those years, Jenna could hardly believe that Tyler liked her just the way she was.

They'd made love in his suite again last night. And it was perfect. No video tapes, no leather, though she'd worn her laciest underwear. And Tyler seemed to like it.

He'd asked about Boston again, her university years, her business, her plans and aspirations.

She hadn't mentioned Brandon, because it had seemed sacrilegious to bring up his name while she was being held in Tyler's arms. But, she'd told him about her and Candice's struggle to put money together to open their own firm.

He seemed impressed by that, and he sure seemed to empathize with their desire to make it on their own. And despite her and Tyler's plans to be quick and dishonorable, they'd talked well into the night.

Again, it had been an early morning with plenty of research and sketching on the agenda. So, by the time she and Candice met with Derek in the afternoon, Jenna was pretty much running on adrenaline.

Derek had offered to get them a hotel meeting room, but Candice said she preferred to sit in a corner of the lobby. She told Derek that she wanted to be able to demonstrate some of their ideas for that space.

Jenna wondered if Candice was just being contrary. Judging by Derek's expression, that's exactly what he thought, too.

"Demographically speaking," said Candice, after they'd set out copies of their presentation. "Your clientele are now coming from Europe and the Far East. The colonial look worked well when you were catering to domestic clients. But, due to advances in air travel, the modern world is shrinking—"

"You don't say," Derek drawled. "You planning to include a fascinating dissertation on the global economy?"

Candice gritted her teeth. "You want me to cut to the chase?"

"Please."

She flipped open the presentation to the first sketch. "You'll see a lot of clean lines," she said tartly. "Muted color. The restrained use of ornamentation. We've flipped ostentatious on its ear to come up with an international flare which will fundamentally change the face of the Quayside hotel."

Derek stared at the drawings without speaking.

Jenna rubbed her damp hands together on top of the table, growing nervous about Candice's hostility.

"Have I done something to offend you?" Derek asked Candice, looking up from the drawings.

"Of course not."

"Then why the witch edge? I'm here to help you, you know."

Jenna jumped in. "And we appreciate you taking time out of your busy schedule to—"

Derek smiled kindly at her, and clasped the top of her hands for a second. "It's not you."

"Of course it's not *her*," said Candice in a sharp tone that shocked Jenna. Candice's professionalism was normally above reproach. It was the cornerstone of their business. What on earth was wrong with her?

"Were you by any chance spoiled as a child?" he asked.

"Did you by any chance get a Rolls for your sixteenth birthday?"

"My fourteenth. It came with a driver. Got a problem with that?"

"About the drawings," said Jenna, flipping to the next page which showed the new concepts for the lobby. "If you'll glance up at the stained glass—"

"That's what I thought," said Candice.

"The structural pillars will have to stay, of course," Jenna continued, hoping against hope to draw their attention away from the argument. Derek had given them this contract. Presumably, he could take it away just as easily. She had no idea why Candice had decided to play with fire.

She valiantly continued. "But, we're going to experiment with a new polymer coating, which…"

"What makes you think you know so much about me?" Derek asked Candice.

"I know your type," said Candice.

"And what type is that?" asked Derek.

Jenna stopped talking and sat back in her chair.

"King of the world," said Candice.

He smiled, crossing his arms over his chest. "I kind of like that image. Does it come with a castle?"

"I'm sure you could buy and sell just about any castle you wanted."

Jenna surreptitiously scooted the drawings under his nose. "The pillars," she whispered.

Derek finally looked down.

"The pillars will have a new polymer coating," said Jenna in a small voice.

"We're upsetting Jenna," Derek said to Candice. "She thinks we're really mad at each other."

"We are," said Candice.

"Maybe," said Derek. "But I'm not going to let that interfere with the contract. It's not Jenna's fault her partner is a spoiled brat."

Candice's jaw dropped open.

"The drawings are fine," Derek said to Jenna. He quickly flipped through the pages. "In fact, they're terrific. Present them to Henry tomorrow. I'm sure he'll be impressed."

TYLER COULD *NOT* believe his eyes.

He blinked a couple of times, hoping the image would disappear. But it didn't.

There.

Right across the lobby.

His big brother was holding court with Jenna and Candice.

Had he not told Derek to stay away from them? Had he not warned his brother about the danger of blowing his cover? What on earth did Derek think he was up to?

While Tyler watched, Jenna gathered her drawings from the small, round table and returned them to her portfolio case.

His eyes narrowed as he realized they had to be the hotel drawings the women were working on yesterday. Why would Derek be looking at the hotel drawings? Surely to goodness he wasn't still stringing them along about decorating his house. And even if he was, how were the hotel sketches relevant to that?

Unless they'd connected Derek to the hotel. Unless they somehow knew Derek was a major shareholder.

Tyler reached up to grip the archway, as yesterday's conversation with Jenna and Candice struck his brain like a lightening bolt. Henry had hired an unknown decorating firm.

Henry would never hire an unknown firm without a recommendation from someone, or pressure from someone. Tyler's fingers tightened on the wood casing. Canna Interiors didn't get the contract because Candice's family intervened. They got the contract because *Derek* intervened.

It all made perfect sense—perfectly horrible sense.

Derek went to Canna Interiors. Then Jenna got a plum contract at the Quayside. And, suddenly, Tyler had a place to live. Henry had even insisted he take a luxury suite.

No wonder Derek was taking a more hands-on approach with the hotel. It wasn't at their father's request. Derek was overseeing the major renovation that *he* had ordered.

The man was absolutely diabolical.

And Tyler was in very big trouble.

If Jenna found out he and Derek were brothers, she was going to start asking questions. She'd assume Tyler had something to do with the contract, and that could lead her straight to his deal with Brandon.

Tyler could *not* let that happen.

He waited, fists clenched, while the women packed up their drawings. As soon as they were clear of the lobby, he stalked across the floor to pounce on his brother.

"What part of *butt out of my life* does this family fail to understand?" he growled, yanking out a high-backed armchair and dropping down across from Derek.

"Problem, bro?" asked Derek, casually signaling the waitress for coffee.

"Don't *bro* me. *You* gave Jenna the decorating contact."

"Guilty as charged," said Derek, not looking the least bit repentant. "I thought it was a stroke of genius."

Tyler rocked back. He'd expected Derek to deny it.

"You gave an unknown decorating firm a multi-million dollar contract so that *I'd* have a hotel suite?" Tyler spread his arms wide in disbelief.

"The hotel needed a facelift. I liked what I saw in their portfolio."

And, Derek, with his typical elbows-out, damn-the-torpedoes approach to business management and life in general, hadn't stopped to consider the consequences. He'd just moved and shaken people and things to suit his impulsive needs.

"Do you have any idea what she's going to do to me when she finds out?" Tyler leaned across the table, practically shouting.

"How's she going to find out?" Derek paused while the waitress set out coffee cups and began filling them. "You report to Brandon, collect the money and get yourself a decent apartment for goodness' sake, and life goes on." Derek dropped a cube of sugar into his coffee cup.

"It's not that simple," said Tyler. It could have been that simple. It should have been that simple. But, suddenly, nothing in his life felt simple.

"Why not?" Derek put into the silence.

"She's..." Tyler sat back in his chair, letting his breath hiss out.

"Engaged, Tyler." Derek's expression grew hard.

"Not really."

"Oh no, you don't." Derek shook his head. "I *knew* that kiss in the spa spelled trouble."

"It's none of your business."

"This is a recipe for disaster." Derek leaned for-

ward. "This is a woman who's marrying for money.
Do *not* let her take you in."

"Nobody's taking me in."

"She might appear all sweetness and light on the
outside, but she's a professional gold digger. It's what
she does." Derek stirred the sugar into his cup.

"Well, she doesn't even know that I have money."

"You sure about that?"

"How would she know?" Jenna knew him as Tyler
Carter, ordinary security guard. She didn't know
about his family.

"There are a million ways to find out who's who in
this town," said Derek, sounding cynical.

"I'm the one deceiving *her*," Tyler pointed out.
"Not the other way around."

"Another good reason to keep your heart out of it."

"My heart has nothing to do with this."

"It's just a fling?"

"Right."

"Then you'll leave at the end of the week, and
she'll never find out we're brothers."

Tyler paused. Leave Jenna at the end of the week?
As in, two days from now? Why did that suddenly
seen incomprehensible?

Derek tapped his spoon on the rim of the cup and
set it down in the saucer. "If you're planning to see
her again, then you've got a *way* bigger problem than
having me as a brother." He crossed his arms over his
chest. "What exactly *are* you reporting to her fiancé,

since the only person she seems to be cheating with is you?"

"She doesn't have to find out that I'm working for Brandon." Even as he said the words, Tyler knew he was grasping at straws. "Brandon will have no reason to tell her," Tyler continued doggedly, ignoring the mounting complications, ignoring the buildup of lies. "I'll file my report, and he'll break it off. End of story."

"Just what fantasy land are you living in, little brother?"

"It'll work." Tyler needed to believe it could all work out. Except for Derek. He had absolutely no idea how he was going to explain Derek away.

"Lying is no way to start off a serious relationship," said Derek.

"Like you're the expert."

"I don't have to be an expert. This is not rocket science."

"What's not rocket science?" Jackson Reeves-DuCarter appeared beside the table, staring down at his two sons, a patented look of disapproval on his weathered face.

"Dad?" Tyler shifted back in his chair, wondering how much his father had overheard.

"Hey, Dad," said Derek with a nod. "Tyler and I were just talking about love."

"Love?" their father snorted, taking the empty seat at the table.

A waitress magically appeared with a huge smile and a cup of coffee for Jackson. The lobby staff obviously knew who was in their midst.

Perfect. Tyler's cover was precarious enough without this.

"We concluded that we're both married to our careers. If you're looking for grandchildren, Striker's your best hope." Derek referred to their middle brother, who was a pilot for the Reeves-DuCarter corporate jet.

"Your mother's not going to be too happy about that," said Jackson.

"We'll work on Striker," said Derek.

"What's this I'm hearing about a renovation project?" Jackson asked Derek, and Tyler just *knew* his life was about to unravel before his eyes.

"Up and coming firm called Canna Interiors is doing the hotel," said Derek. "I discovered them and referred them to Henry."

Tyler waited to hear his father's reaction to Derek's unilateral decision. Derek was definitely the heir apparent. But their father had always ruled the conglomerate with an iron fist.

Jackson nodded, glancing around the lobby. The staff reacted to his interest by immediately looking busy. To that point, they'd been covertly studying his every move.

"Probably about time," he said, shocking Tyler.

That was it? Derek intended to spend several million dollars and his father barely batted an eye?

"We have a problem," said Jackson, setting his coffee cup down on the table.

There. This was more like it. Derek's goose was going over the flames now. Though Tyler had to grudgingly admire his brother's cool demeanor.

Not that Tyler wanted there to be a problem with Canna Interiors. Definitely not. He wanted Jenna and Candice to succeed with this contract. They'd worked hard. They deserved it.

He sat up straighter in his chair, wondering how he could possibly intervene on their behalf if it came down to it.

"Hammond Electronics," said Jackson.

Tyler snapped to attention at the mention of the Hammond name.

"What's the problem?" asked Derek.

"They underbid us on the Ushi contract."

Derek let out a slow whistle through his teeth. "How the hell did that happen? Our numbers were tight. Really tight."

"They're taking a big financial hit, near as I can tell," said Jackson. "Problem is—"

"Without Ushi, we've got no leverage to roll out the overseas wireless network next year. Which will hit profits in the Chinese sector and bring share prices down."

"Right," said Jackson. "Pharmaceuticals will prop

us up for the first quarter. But, after that, the share-holders are going to get nervous."

"We need to cut a deal with Hammond," said Derek.

Tyler raked a hand through his hair. His life was turning into a bad soap opera.

Jackson nodded. "But it needs to be discreet. There's no way we can walk through the front door and start formal negotiations. Somehow, some way, we need an in with the power brokers. The family."

Derek swore under his breath. "I have no idea how the hell we do that. I can't see Charlie or Sean inviting me over to the mansion for drinks."

Tyler blinked at his brother. For a business genius, he was sure slow on the uptake. Candice Hammond...Hammond Electronics. The woman he'd been talking to not ten minutes ago.

Tyler supposed he could play the family hero and introduce his father to Candice. That ought to get them all an invitation for tea, where they could talk electronic deals off the record. Too bad it would destroy what was left of Tyler's life in the process.

Good thing his family didn't really need his help.

Tyler knew that the Reeves-DuCarter accountants rang alarm bells every few days. And, he had complete faith that his family of international business sharks would find a way around this problem. Then they'd discover a brand-new problem by next week.

"I'll leave it with you for now." Jackson stood up. "Nice seeing you, Tyler."

"Dad." Tyler nodded.

His father's personal assistant appeared out of nowhere. Just like the waitress. Amazing how that worked.

As their father walked away, Tyler turned to Derek. "Know what you're going to do?" He wanted to know if Derek had made the Candice connection.

Interested gazes from the staff followed Jackson as he made his way to the front door where he stopped to speak with Henry.

"Do about what?" asked Derek. His expression didn't betray a thing. But then Derek was poker-faced at the best of time.

"About the Hammonds," Tyler pressed.

Derek shrugged. "Not so far. You'll have to give me an hour or so." He took a sip of coffee. "Why do you suddenly care about Reeves-DuCarter?"

Tyler shrugged in return, watching closely, waiting for the significance of the Hammond name to penetrate. If it didn't, he'd have to tell him before it was too late.

Surely to goodness Jenna had introduced Candice using her full name. It was on the back of their brochure if Derek had cared to look closely.

"Better get to work," said Derek, pushing away, not a flicker of recognition on his face.

Tyler was grateful. But he was also beginning to lose faith in his older brother.

9

JENNA'S STOMACH was one huge knot of tension as Candice distributed the restaurant sketches to Henry and the six other board members who were reviewing the proposal.

"It's a northern European—" Candice began as they opened their folders.

Out of the corner of her eye, Jenna saw Derek grab Candice's thigh under the table. Candice broke off.

He gave his head a subtle shake. And, to Jenna's surprise, Candice took his advice.

After a few minutes of silence, one of the board members looked up. Curtis was his name, Jenna thought. A small man with glasses and a prematurely balding head.

"Explain to me how we knock holes in the walls of the top floor without compromising the structural integrity of the building?"

Candice glanced at Jenna, clearly lobbing the question over to her.

Derek's hand was still on Candice's thigh. Jenna wondered if the touch had rendered her partner mute.

"The Lighthouse Restaurant was once renovated," said Jenna. "Of course, we'll need a structural engineer's report before proceeding to final design, but I've inspected the walls up there, and it appears there were once more windows than you have now. We won't be altering the structure from its original design, we'll be retrofitting it to *meet* its original design."

"Where will you get this furniture?" asked another board member.

Since Candice didn't jump in, Jenna continued. "The particular style in that sketch is Autumn Wind. It's designed by a German company, manufactured in the United States. I can bring in a selection of catalogues when we're ready to sign off on the final design." It was a bit presumptuous to word it that way, but the board's clear interest had Jenna feeling more confident.

"I like the new pillars," said Curtis, the small, balding board member.

"The restaurant is exactly what I had in mind," said Henry. There were nods all around the table, showing the esteem in which Henry's opinion was held.

"The board will have to hold a formal vote, of course." Henry stood up, and Jenna followed suit. "But, I think we've got something we can work with here."

"Thank you," Jenna reached out to shake Henry's

hand across the table. Her smiled included all six board members before she followed Candice and Derek out of the boardroom.

"...groping me under the table like some kind of lecher," Candice hissed on her way through the boardroom door.

"I was afraid you'd open your mouth and blow the whole deal," said Derek as the door swung shut. "You should go with your strengths. Let Jenna do all the talking."

"Why—"

"Candice," Jenna interrupted, staring pointedly at her partner. "We *got* the contract."

Candice stopped. "Oh, my goodness." A grin broke out on her face. "You're right." She grabbed Jenna's arm. "We have to celebrate."

"Absolutely," Jenna agreed.

She turned to Derek. "Will you join us for dinner?" It seemed only fair to invite him. Without Derek, they wouldn't have even known about the contract.

"Jenna..." There was a warning tone in Candice's voice.

Derek grinned as he took in Candice's pained expression. "I'd be delighted," he said, a mischievous gleam in his eyes. "But, I insist on taking the two of you out."

Jenna hesitated. "I'm...uh..." Her time was quickly running out with Tyler. It wasn't like she'd be staying at the hotel once the renovation got under way. And neither of them had said anything about the future. She swallowed. "I was planning to invite a...friend along."

"Tyler Carter," Candice put in.

Derek's expression faltered for just a split second, but he quickly recovered. "By all means. Invite Tyler, too."

"Should we show up in pearls and designer gowns?" drawled Candice.

Derek shot her an exasperated look. "Blue jeans," he said.

"Is that a joke?" asked Candice, crossing her arms over her chest.

"Candice!" Jenna was stunned by her friend's behavior.

"No joke," said Derek. "Meet me in the lobby at six-thirty."

JENNA WAS IN a white terry robe with her wet hair twisted up in a matching towel when a knock sounded on the suite door. Checking the peephole, she smiled. Tyler was waiting on the other side.

She quickly flipped the brass lock and flung open the door. "We got it!" she sang without preamble.

"I know." He whipped a huge bouquet of red roses from behind his back. "I just talked to Henry."

"Oh, my." She stared at the flowers. "They're gorgeous."

Tyler laid them in her arms and she hugged them close, eyes unaccountably misting over at the gift.

"You're the one who's gorgeous." He pulled her into a hug, careful not to crush the flowers. "I am so proud of you."

"Thanks," she whispered against his chest.

"They knocked you down," he continued, rocking slightly. "But you bounced back. You worked hard. And you succeeded."

His words caused a tightening in her chest, his pride a warm glow in her heart.

He didn't care if she had a nose job. He didn't care if her abs were rock hard or if her wardrobe was straight off the runways in Paris. He was celebrating her professional achievement, he was celebrating her for who she was.

She pulled back, reaching up to touch his cheek, hardly believing he could be real.

"You're wonderful," she whispered.

Tyler wrapped his hands around her lapels, stroking his thumbs along the looped fabric. "And, you're kind of fuzzy," he teased, bending to give her a kiss on the mouth.

"You like fuzzy?" she asked with a grin.

"I love fuzzy," he said solemnly, staring deeply into her eyes as the clock in the corner struck six.

Her heart gave a little lurch, and she sucked in a quick breath. Without breaking eye contact, he lifted the rose bouquet from between them and set it on a small table in the entry area of the suite.

"As much as lace?" She kept her tone light, not allowing herself to get pulled into the emotion of the moment.

"Better than lace." He reached down and began loosening her belt. "Very prevalent male fantasy, you know. White terry cloth."

She reached up to pat the towel wrapped around her head. "Then you must be fair to bursting with passion."

"Fair to bursting," he agreed, slipping his cool hands beneath her robe, settling them at the small of her back and pulling her close.

"I'm afraid we're going out for dinner," she apologized, leaning against him and inhaling deeply. Musk and a hint of spiced aftershave combined to form the scent she was growing to know so well.

Despite the fact that they had to leave, she closed her eyes for a second to savor the essence of him.

"Now?" he asked.

"As soon as I get dressed," she confirmed with a reluctant nod.

"Forget dinner," he whispered, letting his lips trail along the outside of her ear, brushing his cheek up against hers. "And forget getting dressed. Let's celebrate the contract."

"We can't." His lips did amazing things to her skin,

and she was *so* tempted. Her voice turned breathless. "We're meeting Candice and Derek."

"Derek?" Tyler took a step back, sliding his hands from her waist, pulling them out from beneath her robe. He cocked his head sideways, blue eyes narrowing.

"Derek Reeves," she clarified. "I'm not sure what his title is. But, he's given us a lot of help."

Tyler didn't answer, just stared at her in silence.

"He helped us get the original contract."

"I see."

"Have you met him?"

"Once or twice."

"That's good." She forced herself to back away from Tyler's tempting embrace. "I have to get dressed. We're meeting them in the lobby at six-thirty."

"Sure." Tyler nodded, looking a little annoyed.

"Later?" she asked, making the invitation clear in her voice, afraid she might have upset him.

He smiled, but the tension didn't completely disappear from his expression. "Definitely later," he affirmed.

He wasn't Brandon, she reminded herself, tamping down the butterflies in her stomach as she headed for the bedroom. He was Tyler—emotionally stable and congenial. He wasn't going to fly off the handle over a little thing like inconvenient dinner plans.

TYLER WALKED through the arched gates leading into the amusement park, holding Jenna by the hand.

He could do this. It wouldn't be so bad.

He was simply falling fast and hard for the engaged woman he was spying on, while double dating with his brother—whom he wasn't supposed to know—and who didn't realize the woman beside him was the daughter of his archrival.

"It's an amusement park," Candice observed in an incredulous voice, tipping her head back to stare at the giant Ferris wheel. "*What* are we doing at an amusement park?"

"We're about to be amused," Derek drawled, taking a long look at Candice's high heels and stocking-clad legs. "I *told* you to wear jeans."

Candice frowned at Derek as she scuffed along the pavement in her platform shoes.

Tyler glanced at Jenna's sensible loafers, navy slacks and short-sleeved blouse. It looked like she'd taken his brother seriously when he gave out the dress code.

"I thought you were...joking," said Candice, skirting a bouncing, multicolored balloon which had obviously escaped from a child's grasp.

A huckster from a nearby game booth encouraged customers to try their luck knocking down wooden milk bottles, while the sound of carnival music and children's screams blared from an accelerating circular ride. The smell of cotton candy permeated the breeze.

"Who's up for the bumper cars?" asked Derek, his grin growing wider than those of the orange-pop mustached kids dashing by.

"I am," said Jenna, skipping a step forward. "I haven't been on a ride since the Minnesota state fair when I was a kid."

"I'm not exactly..." Candice glanced worriedly down at her dress.

"Don't be a spoilsport." Derek tucked her arm in the crook of his elbow, firmly steering her toward the ticket booth. "You ignore the dress code, you live with the consequences."

"You let me think you were planning to show off by taking us to a five star restaurant," she protested, trotting to keep up with Derek's longer strides, while obviously trying to free her arm.

"Why would I do that? I believe my exact words were 'wear jeans.'"

"You knew I wouldn't believe you." Candice's voice faded into the noise of the crowd as they grew farther away.

"Bumper cars?" asked Tyler, turning to look at Jenna.

"My favorite," said Jenna, linking her arm with his and steering him after Derek and Candice.

"This wasn't exactly what I had in mind when we talked about celebrating," he muttered, thinking about his big bed back at the hotel and Jenna's smooth skin. Not to mention her purring voice and the taste of her kisses.

"Humor me, and I'll take you through the tunnel of love later on."

"That sounds more like it."

"I'll even kiss you in the dark."

He grunted. "That goes without saying." Then he leaned down close to her ear as they came up on the end of the ticket lineup. "And, I'll cop a feel."

"Pervert," she whispered.

"And you love it."

"Says who?"

"Think they have a house of mirrors?"

She turned to stare at him, eyes widening, cheeks suddenly flushed, and her mouth puckering up in a silent exclamation. The shrieks of the teenagers diminished as the ride next door slowed down.

"Sorry. Sorry," he quickly muttered, forgetting how self-conscious she could be about her sexuality. They really needed to work on that.

"It's okay," she said, composing her expression and smoothing her French braid.

The line moved forward.

"I didn't mean to embarrass you."

"You didn't." She sounded sincere.

"Then, why..." Comprehension dawned, and a slow smile curved his lips.

"I turned you on." He slipped his arm around her waist, tugging her to his side.

"Did not." She struggled to extricate herself.

"*Sure* I did."

"You in line, or what?" a man behind them prompted.

Tyler glanced up and moved forward. Derek and Candice had already bought their tickets and were standing to one side.

"Sex talk turns you on, farm girl."

"It does not." She compressed her lips into a flat line as they moved up to the wicket.

Tyler just grinned and winked at her. He didn't need to argue about it. He fully intended to prove his point in the tunnel of love.

"Two for the bumper cars," said Tyler to the gum-cracking teenager behind the glass. "And four for the tunnel of love." He slipped a twenty through the opening.

"I doubt Derek and Candice will be interested in the tunnel of love," said Jenna.

"What have you got on under that blouse?" he whispered, picking up the tickets.

"Stop."

"Wearing a bra?"

She shot him a cutting look as they rejoined Candice and Derek.

"How can I get into one of those things in this tight

dress?'' asked Candice, nodding worriedly toward the bumper cars.

Tyler surreptitiously ran his fingertips along the back of Jenna's blouse, leaning over to whisper in her ear. ''Nope. No bra.''

''What's that little bro—'' Derek broke off the question midword, and Tyler's heart rate leapt.

''Stop it,'' Jenna whispered to Tyler.

''This way to the bumper cars,'' Derek quickly sang out in an effort to cover his slip. But Tyler could have sworn there was a chuckle in his voice. Easy for him to laugh. His life wasn't hanging in the balance.

Jenna elbowed Tyler in the ribs as they walked. ''Behave,'' she whispered.

''Not a chance. This is way too much fun.'' Thank goodness Derek's slip up had gone unnoticed.

''You are *not* turning me on,'' she said.

Tyler just grinned. He rubbed the smooth back of her blouse between her shoulder blades. ''Well, you're sure turning me on,'' he said in an undertone. ''What about panties?''

She glared at him.

''Just tell me the color.''

She got a little gleam in her eye as they climbed the platform steps to the bumper cars. ''Black.''

''Be still my beating heart.''

''Lace.''

''Tell me more.''

''Thong.''

"I'm yours for life."

"You are *so* easy."

"Here you go." He grasped her hand and helped her into a waiting car. "I'll give you a head start."

"Want me to lift you in or what?" Derek asked Candice as she struggled to step over the edge of a shiny gold car.

"Don't be ridicu—" She stumbled in her high heels, and Derek quickly caught her in his arms.

"I don't need a head start," said Jenna, grasping the small steering wheel and accelerating smoothly away from the platform.

"I grew up driving a tractor," she called over her shoulder.

While Tyler had grown up in the back of a limo. Not the best place to learn anything about the demolition derby. Now Striker, who'd been caught drag racing more than once as a teenager, would excel at bumper cars.

It occurred to Tyler that he might be outclassed on this ride. But, if it was Jenna's favorite, he was definitely willing to give it his best shot. He hopped into a car and took off after her.

A couple dozen shiny vehicles cruised around on several hundred square feet of polished floor space. Tyler dodged child drivers, other adults and teens shrieking over the sound of tinny rock music about three decades out of date.

He chased Jenna down and playfully nudged her car from behind.

Over to his left, Candice showed no such desire for caution. Having been plunked unceremoniously into the car by Derek, she appeared to be taking out her frustration by ramming into the side of his vehicle. That was, until he turned on her and trapped her in a corner.

"Is that all you've got?" Jenna called to Tyler, pulling a hard left and coming around beside him. She sideswiped him, sending him into the wall. His body rocked into the padded door.

With a delighted laugh, she stuck out her tongue and glided away.

That did it. Tyler pulled it into Reverse, swerved around two teenage girls and lit out after Jenna. She ducked in behind a family who were stopped in three separate cars—the man gesturing instructions to his children and his wife.

But Tyler had enough time duck around the other way, avoid a support pillar, and catch Jenna, hitting her head on, then pushing her back toward the wall.

"I've got you where I want you, now," he said.

"This is it?" she asked, grinning. "This is your fantasy?"

"Not hardly. But it's a start."

She suddenly pulled her wheel and slipped out, scooting past him.

"Hey, Candice," she called. "Want some help?"

Before Candice could answer, Jenna rammed the side of Derek's car, dislodging him. "Go, go, go," she called to Candice.

With a huff, Candice drove away.

"Cut her off," Derek called to Tyler.

But Tyler wasn't about to help his brother. Derek could chase down his own women. Tyler had his sights set on Jenna.

He managed to send her into a couple of great spins. But, she gave back as good as she got, outmaneuvering him and then catching his back corner with her bumper. She laughed delightedly at his predicament as the cars turned silent and the ride came to an end.

For her part, Candice kept Derek trapped in a corner for most of the ride time, delivering some kind of scathing lecture that Tyler couldn't hear. Derek responded to her with a dire expression and terse words of his own.

But, after the power died, Candice grudgingly thanked him as he helped her out. She tugged at the hem of her skirt as she headed carefully up the stairs to the exit platform.

"Hate to meet up with you in a tractor," Tyler said to Jenna as they made their way through the exit archway.

"Never mess with me on the farm," she retorted.

"I'm willing to mess with you anytime, anywhere," he whispered back.

"Tunnel of love next," said Jenna in a loud voice.

"Works for me," said Tyler.

"You guys go ahead," said Candice.

"But we bought you tickets, too." Tyler held them out to Derek.

Derek frowned.

"You're not scared to be alone with her, are you?" Tyler teased, remembering her recent diatribe.

"Of course I'm scared," Derek retorted. "She'll probably throw me into the canal."

Tyler grinned at the image of five-foot-six, 110-pound Candice tossing Derek the linebacker anywhere.

"A canal, you say?" asked Candice sweetly, whisking the tickets out of Tyler's hand. "I'm not usually vindictive. But I can make exceptions."

"Them's fightin' words," said Derek.

"Do you think it's safe to leave them alone together?" asked Jenna.

"Derek won't hurt her," Tyler answered.

"That's not what I'm worried about," she said falling into step beside him as they headed for the flashing red sign that advertised the tunnel of love.

"Let Derek take care of himself. This is the tunnel of love. Your job is to focus on me." He jammed his thumb against his puffed up chest as they stopped behind Derek and Candice at the back of the line.

"I've never been through a tunnel of love," said

Jenna, craning her neck to look around the other people in the lineup.

"Didn't have one at the state fair?" asked Tyler.

"I was a kid back then."

"So, this is your first time?" he whispered meaningfully in her ear as the line moved forward onto the steep, blue ramp. "I'm honored." He maneuvered Jenna in front of him between the looped chain fence, resting his hands lightly on her shoulders.

"As well you should be." She sniffed and stuck her nose in the air.

He chuckled as the attendant took their tickets. Then he slipped his hand into hers as they stood beside the man-made canal waiting for the next car. Derek and Candice disappeared through the doors into the dark tunnel.

Tyler tightened his fingers around Jenna's hand, steadying her as she stepped into the rocky boat. Then he ducked under the striped canvas canopy and settled on the padded bench seat beside her.

As the swinging wooden door thumped shut behind them, he slipped an arm around her shoulders, pulling her close, leaning his head against the top of hers and inhaling the scent of her rose shampoo. "This is much better than bumper cars."

The theme from *Love Story* played softly in the background, and a muted, colored light show began to flash hearts against the tunnel wall. The water lapped hollowly on the sides of the little covered car, which was pulled silently along underwater.

Derek and Candice were ahead of them, out of sight in the darkness.

Jenna sighed and settled her head on Tyler's shoulder. "This is nice. But nothing's better than bumper cars."

He chuckled and wrapped his free hand around her rib cage, stroking his thumb beneath her unbound breast. "Afraid I have to disagree on that one. You've got it all over bumper cars." He kissed her temple.

"Are you going to talk sexy now?"

"You bet."

"Okay." She straightened, smoothing her hands across her slacks. "I'm ready. Go for it."

"You don't need to brace yourself," he said. She was a deeply sexy and sensual woman. He didn't know why she fought it so darn hard. "Just relax."

"I am relaxed."

"Tell you what," said Tyler. "Why don't you go first."

"First?"

"Yeah."

"Me?"

"Sure."

"Is this quid pro quo?"

"Absolutely."

"What am I supposed to say?"

"Say anything you want. I can guarantee you'll turn me on." Tyler settled back, closing his eyes.

"But..."

"Go ahead. Say something sexy."

"You sure?"

"I'm sure."

"Okay." She nuzzled her face up to his ear, voice dropping to a husky whisper. "I'm naked under my clothes."

Tyler waited. And waited some more as her soft breathing puffed against his neck.

"That's it?" he asked.

She shrugged. "That's all I can think of at the moment. Your turn."

"You have a lot to learn about—"

There was a sudden splash some distance in front of them, and they both rocked forward, peering into the dark water. Flashing lights rebounded off the shiny surface.

"You don't suppose..." Tyler ventured.

"She wouldn't," said Jenna, still staring into the water.

"Derek?" Tyler called.

"Yeah?" A faint response came back to them.

"You okay?"

"Oh, for God's sake." The voice was stronger this time. "I'm not sure what it was. Besides, what do you think she could do to me?"

"Nothing," Tyler called, biting off a laugh. "Never mind."

He sat back in the seat, drawing Jenna with him. "Where were we?"

"You were going to show me how sex talk is done."

"Ah. Right." He smoothed her hair back from her forehead, kissing her lightly on the temple, savoring the warmth and texture of her skin. "It's all about evoking a fantasy. Telling the other person your intimate thoughts. Making them feel like they're along for the ride, even if you're not really doing anything."

He let his cheek come to rest against her. "For example, when I close my eyes at night, I picture you in my bed. All naked and warm and soft."

He stroked his hand down her opposite cheek, pressing her against him. "Your skin is like silk, and you smell of roses." Like she did now. He closed his eyes.

Of it's own accord, his voice dropped to a whisper. "I never realized how much I loved roses until you brought their scent into my life."

She relaxed against him with a soft sigh, and he suddenly realized that all the lonely nights of his life were merely a foil for her. If he'd never been alone, he wouldn't appreciate the absolute ecstasy of finally holding her close.

"I imagine I can hear your breathing," he continued, sinking into the fantasy he'd experienced night after night since the first day he'd met her.

"I feel your heartbeat." He shifted so that his forehead was touching her hair, creating a little cocoon of air that was all her, all him. "Your body warms the cold places in my heart. Places I never even knew existed."

He kissed her neck, tasting her skin, pulling her closer. "While we make love, I taste you, inhale you. Feel you pulsating through my bloodstream, and I can't tell where you end and I begin."

His arms tightened inexorably around her, and he moved to kiss her mouth. Then he pulled back, staring into her eyes, the gold flecks sparkled in the muted lights. He felt as though he was stepping off a cliff into outer space.

"I imagine my soul inside you, and I know I want to keep it there...forever." His words dropped off into silence, and their breathing synchronized.

"Wow," she whispered.

Wow, his brain echoed.

Their little boat burst through the exit doors into the lights and noise and motion of the midway.

10

"LADIES' ROOM," Candice ordered, grabbing Jenna by the arm, all but hauling her out of the tunnel of love boat.

Jenna blinked in surprise for a second, before following Candice.

"What did you do to Candice?" Tyler pasted his brother with an accusing stare as the two women headed off across the park.

"Me?" Derek looked affronted. "Nothing." But his jaw tightened and his eyes narrowed as he watched Candice's retreating back. Then he pivoted on his heel, heading in direction of the arcade games.

"So, what was that splash?" Tyler pressed, falling into step beside his brother.

"You think I'd actually throw a woman into the canal?"

"I don't know what you'd do. You're renovating a damn hotel to keep me from living in my office."

"I'm renovating the hotel because it needs a renovation."

Tyler paused, debating which tack to follow, deciding the hotel argument could wait. "Why is Candice upset?" he asked.

Derek came to a halt in front of a football game stall. He tossed a five-dollar bill on the counter, receiving four footballs for his money. "You mean Candice Hammond?"

"Right."

"Candice Hammond Electronics Division."

Tyler couldn't help the smile that crept out. "One and the same."

"Why the hell didn't you tell me?"

"Same reason you didn't tell me I was being handed a luxury suite under false pretenses."

"Well, imagine my surprise—" The first ball left Derek's hand like a rocket, knocking down the whole stack of wooden milk bottles "—when I realized I was kissing Chuck Hammond's daughter."

"You kissed her? Does she know who you are?"

"I kissed her." Derek lined up another football with the next stack of bottles. "And no, she doesn't."

"Last time I checked you two were at each other's throats."

"Yeah, well, we got over it." Bam. Another stack came crashing down, to the stunned amazement of the operator. "Sort of."

Tyler had seen the wooden bottle game exposed on PBS. One of the bottom bottles was always heavier than the rest, making it all but impossible to knock down. But Derek's arm was obviously up to the challenge.

"Did she kiss you back?" he asked, less interested in the physics of a carnival game than his brother's exploits with Candice.

"Hard to tell." Derek tossed the fourth ball with stunning success.

"You couldn't *tell?* But... Never mind."

The attendant put a big purple stuffed horse on the counter beside Derek. The music changed on the ride next door, and Derek pulled out another five.

"In the end, yeah, I'd say she did. Reluctantly." He tossed another football. "My approach would have been a whole hell of a lot different if I'd known who she was." He turned to glare at Tyler.

Tyler held up his hands. "I'm just a disinterested bystander. Unlike some members of this family, I don't meddle in other people's lives."

"I don't like surprises, Tyler. You had an obligation to the family." Derek turned back to the game, lined up and another ball flew from his hand.

"So you and Dad could use her to further your business interests? I don't think so. I like Candice."

"Did it occur to you that she might be a spy?" Derek made another clean sweep, sending four stacks of bottles crashing, this time earning him a gray elephant with a pink bow on its trunk.

"Candice? A spy? The woman's a decorator."

"You don't find it just a little coincidental that her

family underbids us on one of the most pivotal contracts of the decade, and she shows up in our lives the same week?"

Tyler snorted. "You're paranoid." He'd learned a long time ago that the word "pivotal" was hyperbole spouted by Derek and his father. Every business deal was the most *pivotal* of the decade.

"I'm vigilant. That woman could be dangerous."

"That woman is not dangerous. *I'm* the spy," said Tyler. "Jenna and Candice are innocent."

"We already know Jenna's a gold—"

"Don't!" Tyler warned. "She's breaking up with Brandon."

"She told you that?"

"Not in so many words..." She had to break up with Brandon. No woman could make such sweet love to one man and still consider marrying another.

Derek shook his head and slapped another five on the counter.

"Uh..." The teenage attendant hesitantly pointed to a sign that gave him the right to refuse customers.

Derek growled in the kid's direction and was rewarded with four more footballs. He tossed one immediately.

"You," he paused, a ball in his left hand, tapping his finger against Tyler's chest, "file your report to Brandon, then get out of this mess."

"And leave you to pick up the pieces?"

"Exactly." Derek threw the second ball. Strike.

"Listen, big brother."

Derek threw another ball.

"Candice did not start a business with Jenna—"

Fourth ball.

"So that Brandon would hire me—"

Slap. Another five on the counter.

"So that you would hire them—"

Next ball.

"So that I could live at the hotel—"

Two in rapid succession.

"So that she could spy on you—"

Last ball.

"To screw up your electronics deal." Tyler inhaled deeply as the attendant added a brown kangaroo to the embarrassingly large stack of stuffed animals.

"Prove it," said Derek.

THE SPACE NEEDLE restaurant had fantastic views of downtown Seattle and Puget Sound. Lights twinkled from the towering office buildings, and a glowing cruise ship slipped between islets out on the calm water.

Jenna slid into a curved booth between Candice, Tyler and a menagerie of enormous stuffed animals destined for the children at the hospital. She let her glance roam back and forth between Derek and Candice.

Neither of them seemed thrilled by the fact that they'd succumbed to a mutual attraction and kissed.

Candice had been positively rattled back at the ladies' room, and Derek was glowering.

They kept a good foot of air space between them on the bench seat, not to mention an elephant, a kangaroo and a giant, long-haired dog.

Jenna on the other hand leaned sideways a little and pressed her shoulder up against Tyler's. His unbelievably sweet words in the tunnel of love echoed back through her brain. She had no idea where their relationship was headed, but so far the ride was the most amazing experience of her life.

The restaurant was crowded. Laughter from the other tables swirled around them. The candle flame dipped as waiters swept by, laden with trays of fresh bread and sizzling seafood in the dimly lit room.

While the cocktail waitress set their drinks down, Jenna linked her fingers with Tyler's under the table. He gave her hand a squeeze and sent her an intimate smile.

"A toast..." said Derek, raising his scotch glass, gazing contemplatively into its amber depths. Then he glanced at Tyler. "To secrets," he said.

Tyler coughed, and Candice gave Derek a narrow-eyed glare. Derek gazed impassively at Candice for a still, silent moment, as if he was waiting for her to say something.

Tyler's cell phone rang, breaking the strange moment.

"Sorry." He frowned, letting go of Jenna's hand

while he retrieved the phone from his shirt pocket. "I forgot to turn it off." He flipped it open. "Yeah?"

His listened for a second, then his eyes widened and the blood drained from his face. "How did you get—"

He drummed his fingers on the tablecloth. "No. Not now. I'll have to call you back."

Then his fingers stilled, and he was silent for a moment more, easing ever so slightly away from Jenna. "No," he repeated. "Now is *not* a good time."

He closed his eyes for a second. "Fine. Right."

He hit a button, turned off the phone and set it down on the table.

"Sorry," he said to the group in general, lifting his glass and tossing back a swallow of the single malt. "Where were we?"

"Everything all right?" Jenna asked worriedly. There was obviously a problem with something in his life.

"It's fine," said Tyler, setting down the glass. "Just business." But his tone of voice made it obvious that everything wasn't fine.

"Uh, Tyler?" Now Derek's voice sounded tense and vaguely warning. He gave Tyler a meaningful nod, something obviously transpiring between the two.

Jenna wondered if the men knew each other better than she realized.

Tyler turned his head to look behind him.

Jenna followed the direction of his gaze, not seeing anything out of the ordinary.

"Should we leave?" asked Candice, a puzzled expression on her face that mirrored Jenna's feelings.

"Of course not," said Derek easily. "We'll be right back. Just a little hotel business." He slid smoothly out of the booth.

"Sorry," Tyler said to Jenna, giving her a quick kiss. "I'll be right back."

Candice watched the two men leave. "What on earth was that all about?"

"Business?" Jenna ventured, glancing behind her again, seeing them come to a halt at another table. It wasn't so unusual. After all, they both worked for the hotel.

She turned back to Candice, ignoring the twilight zone feeling.

"Hit star sixty-nine," said Candice, nodding to Tyler's cell phone.

"Forget it." Jenna wasn't about to invade Tyler's privacy, under any circumstances.

"What if it's another woman? What if Derek's in on it?"

"That's a stretch," said Jenna, forcing a note of confidence into her voice. "Derek and Tyler barely know each other."

"I wonder about that." Candice's gaze trailed off behind Jenna's right ear.

"You're being paranoid," said Jenna, ignoring the

fact that she'd wondered exactly the same thing thirty seconds ago. The two men knew each other through work. They were talking business.

"Then what's the harm in hitting star sixty-nine?" Candice shifted closer along the curved seat. "If it's a business call, great. He's in the clear. But if you don't check now, you're always going to wonder."

"I won't wonder," Jenna insisted. "I trust him."

"Get real, Jenna. Fact is, you barely know the man. Maybe he's some kind of con artist."

"He's a security guard. Besides, what would he be after?"

"Your money."

"I don't have money. You have money. Are rich people always this paranoid?"

"I don't have money either," said Candice. "My father has money. My brothers have money." She glanced in the direction of Tyler and Derek. A crease formed between her eyebrows before she turned back to Jenna.

"If you don't hit star sixty-nine, I will." She reached for the telephone.

"No," Jenna protested.

"If you're right, there's no harm done," said Candice. She flipped open the phone and hit the numbers.

Jenna closed her eyes and sighed in defeat, glancing back to where Tyler and Derek were still talking to an older couple, making sure they didn't see Candice commandeer the cell phone.

Candice held it close to Jenna's ear, leaning over so they could both hear.

"This is ridiculous," Jenna muttered.

"Shhh," said Candice.

A stilted computer voice read out the last number called.

Jenna's stomach contracted. She turned to stare at Candice in amazement. "Where did Tyler get Brandon's private number?"

"If you wish to connect to this number," the computer voice continued, oblivious to Jenna's confusion, "press one now."

Candice pressed one.

"You can't!" Jenna tried to grab the phone.

"Jenna," Candice growled. *"Brandon called Tyler."*

"I can't talk to him," said Jenna.

"Of course you can't," said Candice.

"Rice here," came Brandon's voice.

"Hello," said Candice, her voice higher than normal and decidedly nasal. "This is Tyler Carter's secretary calling."

Jenna started to shake. What was going on? How had Tyler found out about Brandon? Why would Brandon call Tyler?

"I don't know anyone named Tyler Carter," said Brandon.

For a second, Jenna was relieved.

"You just called him five minutes ago," said Candice, and Jenna's short-lived relief evaporated.

"You mean Tyler Reeves?"

"Right," said Candice without missing a beat.

Jenna's stomach turned to a ball of lead. Brandon *had* called Tyler. He did know Tyler.

"Mr. Reeves has asked me to call you back and get the particulars," Candice bluffed.

"Particulars?" Brandon barked. "There are no particulars. The final McBride report is due tomorrow, and he'd better make sure I get it before noon if he wants his check."

Jenna gasped. A report? On *her*? That meant...

"Right," said Candice between clenched teeth.

That meant Tyler was the latest in Brandon's string of sleazy P.I.s.

Candice flipped the phone shut.

That meant Tyler was spying on her. It meant she'd bared her soul, and everything else about her, to Brandon's spy.

"I have to get out of here." Jenna gasped for breath. The room started to spin, and there was a roaring in her ears. The lights of downtown Seattle blurred, and the laughter of the other restaurant patrons grated on her raw nerves.

Candice put a hand on her arm. "You okay?"

"Fine." She was anything *but* fine. "I just have to leave."

"You're not going to stay and grill Tyler?"

"No!" Jenna practically shrieked. "What's to ask? He's working for Brandon." She wrapped her arms around her stomach, suddenly cold in the thin blouse.

Tyler's sweet, sexy words. His romantic caresses. His candlelight and wine and uninhibited sex. He was reporting it all back to Brandon.

"Men are scum," said Candice, propping one elbow on the table, shaking her head.

Jenna couldn't put forward one single argument to the contrary.

"Why would he do it?" she asked the air in general. "Did he need a more exciting report? Did Brandon pay him to find out if I'd... Oh, God, Candice. Do you think Brandon *paid* him to sleep with me?"

"No. Jenna, don't. You need to talk to Tyler."

"I can't."

"If you don't, you'll wonder for the rest of your life. And you *sure* deserve a explanation." Candice turned to glare at Tyler's back. "Not to mention a little verbal satisfaction."

"I have to leave," said Jenna, grabbing her purse. "I can't face him."

"He's the one who shouldn't be able to face you."

"I have to go." She just wanted to curl up and die in peace.

Candice nodded, her jaw tight. "Okay. Go ahead. I'll take care of him."

"You're staying?"

"If it's okay with you. I'd really like a little verbal satisfaction."

"Candice, you don't need—"

"Go," said Candice. "Leave him...*them* to me."

"I can't leave you alone... What do you mean *them*?"

"Tyler Reeves. Derek Reeves."

Jenna froze. Amongst all the other stunning revelations, that little detail had slipped right past her. They were related? Brothers?

"What on earth is going on here?" she whispered rhetorically. And how was Brandon behind it?

"Don't worry," said Candice, sitting up straight and squaring her shoulders. "I fully intend to find out. For both of us. I take it you're not going back to the hotel?"

Jenna shook her head, her eyes burning with unshed tears. She was never going back to the hotel.

"The contract," she whispered. Their dream contact. Their great accomplishment. And it was all a sham. It was blowing up in their faces.

"Leave it to me. I'll figure it out." Candice looked every inch a mother lion ready to go into battle. "I'll come over later."

Jenna nodded. With a single, painful glance at Tyler's back, she slid out of the booth and headed for the exit.

Tyler only half listened as his mother talked about family plans for next month. Striker was going to be in town for an entire week, and she was convinced the brothers needed to get together. Fishing, he thought she'd said. Which was odd, since none of them fished.

All he could think about was Jenna. And the close call of Brandon phoning him. And how he hated that there was a lie between them. And how he needed to tell her about the contract with Brandon and tear up the report.

Which meant giving up the money.

Which meant giving up his business.

Which meant he needed a job...in the family firm...giving up the independence he'd worked so long and hard to achieve.

"...up in Canada," his mother was saying. "Striker could fly you all to..." Her voice carried on in the background as Tyler focused in on his father.

Ask him, he told himself. *Just open up your mouth and say you want a job.*

His mother would be thrilled, Tyler knew. And his father wouldn't turn him down. He'd have a steady salary, benefits, regular hours and money—plenty of money. All the things that a man needed if he wanted to impress a woman.

If he wanted to offer her a viable alternative to her rich fiancé.

Just do it.

Tyler opened his mouth.

But nothing came out. He couldn't bring himself to say the words.

He stared at his father's profile. He didn't have anything against Jackson. His father was a fair and honest man. He treated his employees well.

Derek was certainly happy.

Tyler let his gaze slide sideways to his brother. Derek was excited by the family business dealings, engaged, seemingly fulfilled by his job.

Tyler shifted his attention back to his father. Just four little words. "I want a job." That's all it would take.

It wasn't the end of the world. He wouldn't be admitting defeat. It wasn't like P.I. work was all thrills and excitement. Independence was probably an illusion anyway.

As he opened his mouth to seal the rest of his life, he felt something tighten around his throat. It choked off his air. His hand flew to his collar.

"We'll talk at the office on Monday," his father said to Derek.

"I'll clear my morning," Derek responded.

Tyler couldn't bring himself to do it. Independence might be an illusion. But it was *his* illusion. And he loved his illusion.

"Have a nice dinner, boys." Tyler's mother reached out and squeezed his hand. "Drop by to see the Bakers on Tuesday if you can. We're giving them a little anniversary party."

"I'll try," Tyler whispered, automatically leaning down to kiss her perfectly made-up cheek. Even at fifty-five, she hadn't lost any of her beauty and she was still the consummate hostess.

Swallowing around his dry throat, he headed back to his own table. One little report. Only twenty-four more hours. Then, if Jenna didn't break up with Brandon, Brandon was sure to break up with her. Leaving the field clear for Tyler, who would put all this behind him and make his P.I. agency succeed come hell or high water.

"Where's Jenna?" he asked, coming to a halt at the table, taking in the empty seat.

"Sit down, boys," said Candice in a brittle voice. Her narrow eyes pinned Tyler with an accusatory stare. She didn't even spare a glance for Derek, studiously ignoring him where he stood next to her.

Then she spread her arms expansively, banging her elbow into the kangaroo. "And decide which one of you is going to tell me what the hell is going on."

11

TYLER STILLED. His gaze flicked to his brother's face. Derek's expression tightened.

There were moments in a man's life when he knew, deep down in his gut, with dead-dog certainty, that he'd just made a terrible mistake. It had happened the morning his partner Reggie had disappeared. And it was happening again now.

"I know what you're thinking." Candice shifted her attention back and forth between them, manicured fingertips tracing small circles on the white tablecloth. "What do we say? Which lie does she know?"

Tyler felt his heart rate kick up. Which lie *did* she know? Not knowing what else to do, he slipped fatalistically into his seat.

"It's this way," said Candice as Derek folded his body onto the padded bench. "I'm not about to tell you which lies I know. So, you can just start from the top."

Derek picked up his drink and swirled the ice.

Tyler could almost feel his brother's overprotective instincts kick in.

"All right," said Derek. "Fine."

"Derek, don't," Tyler warned, shaking his head. He didn't need his brother to take the fall for him.

Derek ignored him. "I didn't exactly lie," he said to Candice. "I never use Reeves-DuCarter. And I didn't know you were a Hammond until tonight."

Candice glanced over her shoulder at Tyler's parents. Then she squinted at Derek, giving him a cold, assessing half smile. "Didn't know about that one. But, keep talking."

Tyler let out a short, pithy curse.

Candice switched her attention to him. "You have *no* idea."

"Where's Jenna?" he asked. Whatever they knew, whatever had happened, he needed to talk to her right away.

"Not so fast," said Candice, watching Tyler closely as she picked up her long-stemmed glass and took a sip of white wine. "Your turn now."

Derek rocked forward. "Leave him—"

"Quit acting like a mother hen," Candice barked out.

Tyler wracked his brain. What had happened? Did they know about Brandon? How could they suddenly know about Brandon?

"Fine," said Tyler, sitting back, reflexively rubbing rivulets into the condensation on his highball glass with his thumb and index finger, trying to figure out where to start. "I'm a Reeves-DuCarter, too."

"That much, I just figured out," said Candice. She leaned forward, looking hard into Tyler's eyes. "Let's cut to the chase. What I want to know is why the hell is Brandon paying you to sleep with Jenna?"

Adrenaline jerked Tyler's wrist, and he felt his heart plummet straight to his toes. "*Nobody's* paying me to sleep with Jenna."

"Brandon told me he was expecting a report."

"How the hell did you..."

"It's called star sixty-nine." Her gaze flicked to Tyler's cell phone.

"You are some piece of work," said Derek.

"Me?" Candice scoffed at Derek. "You, Brandon and Tyler conspire to manipulate Jenna, and you dare call *me* a piece of work?"

"It's not a conspiracy," said Tyler. "It was a simple surveillance job. Brandon thought she might be..." *Cheating.* It sounded pretty insulting now. Since, as Derek had so aptly put it, the only person Jenna had cheated with was Tyler.

"Thought she might be what?" Candice asked.

"Cheating on him," Tyler reluctantly admitted, unable to look Candice in the eye. His gaze searched the room, hoping Jenna would come back to the table soon. He knew she must be upset.

"How could Jenna be cheating on Brandon?" asked Candice.

"I don't know how flexible you Bostonians are,"

Derek put in sarcastically. "But out West we take our engagements pretty seriously."

"What engagement?"

"*Jenna's* engagement," said Derek.

"Jenna's not engaged."

"With Brandon," said Derek.

"She broke up with Brandon four months ago."

"Broke up?" The air burst from Tyler's lungs. His gaze shot back to Candice. "The bastard *lied* to me."

"He did if he told you he was engaged to Jenna." She gave Tyler a look of disdain. Then her attention immediately returned to Derek. "*Why* on earth did you give us the decorating contract?"

All this time Tyler had been waiting for Jenna to acknowledge her relationship with Brandon, to break up with Brandon. And all this time she wasn't engaged. She was free.

"The hotel needed renovating," said Derek, taking a swallow of his scotch.

"Where is she?" demanded Tyler. He *needed* to get to Jenna.

"And you chose Canna Interiors, because..." Candice ignored Tyler, arching her perfect, condemning eyebrows in Derek's direction.

"So I didn't have to live in my office," Tyler quickly interjected, wanting nothing more than to get the sordid details out on the table so he could start dealing with them. "Now go get Jenna."

"I liked your portfolio," said Derek.

"Live in your office?" Candice appeared to realize that Tyler was still alive.

"I sold my house," said Tyler. "Derek was worried. He wanted me to stay at the hotel. Now tell me where I can find Jenna."

"I *liked* your portfolio." Derek's deep voice rumbled in exasperation.

"You gave us a *multimillion dollar* contract so Tyler could stay at a fancy hotel while he watched Jenna?"

"*I liked your portfolio.*" The words were staccato through Derek's clenched teeth.

"You know…" said Candice, running her finger along the rim of her wineglass. "Jenna would tell you to take the contract and choke on it. But, as it turns out, I'm not Jenna."

"No kidding," said Derek.

"Where *is* Jenna?" Tyler repeated. He had to find her. He had to explain. He had to apologize and beg her forgiveness. He had to change his life.

"The way I see it," said Candice. "I've got a duly executed contract for three-point-five million of your dollars."

Derek stilled.

"And I am going to make sure I spend every last cent."

"Where's Jenna?"

"She left," Candice said to Tyler, without breaking her focus on Derek.

"What do you mean *left?*" asked Tyler.

Derek rested his elbows on the tabletop and leaned toward Candice. "I guess that means I'll have to watch you every single step of the way."

"Left the restaurant?" Tyler demanded.

Candice turned to Tyler, eyes narrowing. "Give me one, single good reason why I should tell you anything."

Tyler froze. He stared at Candice in silence for several heartbeats. The clink of glasses and the buzz of other conversations seemed to rise around them. A freighter horn sounded far below. And the candlelight wavered in front of his eyes.

"Because I can't live without her," he answered honestly, shuddering as powerful emotions coursed through him in a pressure wave. They were stunning in their clarity.

He was in love with Jenna.

Flat-out, body and mind, heart and soul in love with her.

Candice stared back at him, blinking her dark lashes a couple of times. "You might want to use that as your opening line."

He absolutely, positively would use that as his opening line, followed quickly by the fact that he loved her, he was sorry and he'd do anything to make it up to her.

He flipped open his cell phone. Like Jenna and Candice before him, he hit star sixty-nine.

Derek's forehead creased.

"Rice here," came the voice on the other end.

Tyler drummed his fingers on the table top. "Tyler Reeves. I quit."

"Not without giving me a report."

"Watch me."

"You can't quit now."

Tyler's voice was flat, emotionless. "Oh, yes, I can, you lying, cheating son of a—"

"Breach of contract," taunted Brandon.

"Too bad."

"I'll ruin you."

"No," Tyler chuckled dryly, catching Derek's eye. "You won't. But, if you ever, *ever* dare come near Jenna McBride, or try to contact her again, or mess with her life in any way, shape or form, I will bring the entire Reeves-DuCarter International empire down on your head. There won't be a place on the planet for you to hide."

Tyler took the sudden silence at the other end of the line as understanding. He shut off the phone.

"Go, baby brother," whistled Derek.

Tyler stood up.

Derek cocked his head to one side, addressing Candice. "What are the chances of your parents coming to the wedding?"

"What wedding?"

"I have every faith in my little brother here, and there's something I'd like to talk to your father about." Derek's voice faded as Tyler strode to his parents' table.

"Dad?" He slipped into one of the vacant chairs.

"Yes, Tyler?" His father paused between bites of his Greek salad.

Tyler took a deep breath. It felt good. He wasn't confused anymore, and it was easy to breathe this time. "I'd like a job with Reeves-DuCarter."

His father slowly set down his fork and straightened in his chair.

"Tyler?" his mother whispered, pure joy in her voice.

"Are you sure, son?" His father's gray eyebrows slanted together.

"I'm positive," said Tyler, nodding once.

His mother reached out and squeezed his hand. "We couldn't be more delighted, right Jackson?"

"What brought about the change of heart?" asked Jackson.

Tyler didn't mind the question. His father had every right to wonder why he was suddenly interested in the family business.

"I've met a woman."

His mother gasped, and her fingers squeezed tighter on Tyler's hand.

"She's a very, very special woman." That was the understatement of the century. "I don't know if she'll have me, but I need to offer her stability. Derek didn't tell you, but Reggie embezzled from IPS and I'm all but bankrupt."

Amazingly, it felt good to come clean about the whole debacle.

His father nodded. "I know."

"You know?"

"It wasn't Derek or Striker. I heard about it through my own security staff."

"Small city," Tyler acknowledged.

"Where's your young lady?" his mother asked, glancing toward the table where Derek and Candice still sat.

"I upset her," said Tyler. "She left, but I'm going to catch up with her." He'd try the hotel. If that didn't pan out, he'd head for her apartment.

"I don't know if I'll be able to make it better," he said. "But I'm sure going to try."

"You go," said his mother. "You and your father can talk tomorrow."

Tyler glanced at his father. He'd like nothing better than to leave right now.

"Go." Jackson nodded with a smile. "There's a job for you as soon as you're ready. We can iron out the details later."

"Thanks, Dad."

Tyler stood up, feeling lighter than he had in weeks. Jenna was worth anything. She was worth everything.

JENNA SPLASHED cold water on her face, trying to ease the heat and discoloration under her eyes. She'd waited until the Space Needle restroom was empty before emerging from the opulent stall. Now, she reached for a white towel in the basket on the marble counter to dry her face.

Her makeup was ruined, but that was the least of her worries.

Tyler was spying on her.

She'd been spied on before, she told herself as she briskly rubbed her face. It wasn't like this was a new experience. And it wasn't like P.I.s in general had any scruples about how they got close to their subjects.

She dried each finger individually. They wanted the story, and that was all that counted. And Brandon could afford the best, or the worst, depending on how one looked at it....

She tossed the towel into the basket.

Tyler was obviously one of the most thorough.

She glanced in the big mirror, straightening her blouse, smoothing her hair back with her hands. All she had to do was make it down the elevator and hail a cab. Then she'd head home and forget any of this ever happened.

Maybe they'd get the library contract. They would simply have to build up their firm more slowly. The Quayside contract was too good to be true, anyway.

She felt fresh tears burn the back of her eyes.

Every damn thing about it was too good to be true.

She shook her head and picked up her purse, refusing to let the silly tears start afresh. She was not going to let any lying, low-life P.I. do this to her. She was going to be strong.

The brass and oak door opened, and two women walked in. Jenna quickly lowered her head and brushed past them.

She walked swiftly down the carpeted hallway to the octagon shaped lobby where the express elevator would take her back to street level. She kept her focus on the floor in front of her, not wanting to meet anyone's eyes.

"Jenna?" Tyler's voice scraped her raw nerves.

She stopped abruptly.

"Jenna, honey," he repeated.

"No." Her voice was hoarse as she reached for the elevator call button.

"We need to talk."

She shook her head, afraid to try to speak around her thickening throat.

"I can explain." He came closer in the empty lobby. "It's not what you think."

Not what she thought? How could it not be what she thought?

"You lied to me," she choked out.

"I didn't mean—"

"You've done nothing but lie to me and manipulate me since the moment we met."

"I didn't know you then," he whispered. And she

did what she swore she'd never do again. She looked at him. Same sweet face. Same earnest eyes. Same effortless charisma.

"*That's* your explanation?" she asked, fighting the remnants of her attraction to him. "It's okay to ruin a woman's life if you don't know her?"

"I didn't know—"

"You *slept* with me."

He nodded. "I know."

"You knew me well enough to sleep with me, but not well enough to be honest."

He closed his eyes and shook his head. "I was wrong."

"You got that right."

Two more couples emerged from the restaurant as the elevator bell pinged.

"Leave," said Jenna.

"I can't," said Tyler.

"I don't want to talk to you," she ground out in an undertone as the couples came closer.

He bent to speak close to her ear. "I don't blame you."

He straightened, raking his fingers through his short hair as the elevator doors opened.

Jenna walked inside. She wasn't going to listen to him this time. He was too slick, too suave, too quick to come up with a story. She couldn't trust him.

Tyler and the two couples followed her in.

Jenna stood stiffly as it whisked them to the ground.

She didn't even know why he was bothering. Surely to goodness he had plenty to report to Brandon. Surely to goodness, Brandon would now realize their relationship was over.

Now, there was a positive.

Her heart might be shredded into a million pieces, and she might never be able to trust another man as long as she lived, but at least she wouldn't have to worry about Brandon anymore.

She should thank Tyler for that.

She quickly raised her hand to her mouth as a bubble of hysterical laughter tried to form.

Thankfully, the elevator doors swept open, and she practically ran into the main floor lobby.

"Wait." Tyler paced along beside her.

She shook her head and walked faster. "No way."

"I need to talk to you."

"I won't listen."

"I thought you were *engaged* to him."

Jenna slowed a notch and glanced sideways at Tyler. "I'm not."

"I know that now. But I didn't then."

"Let me see if I'm understanding your ethics correctly." Despite her resolve, she came to a stop and turned to face him. Maybe Candice was right. Maybe she did need a little verbal satisfaction.

The lobby was mostly empty.

"You have no problem spying on and lying to an engaged woman that you don't know," said Jenna.

"I'm a private eye."

"So what?"

"It's my job."

"You sleep with everyone you spy on."

"Of *course* not."

"How'd I get so lucky?"

"Jenna, please."

"Is there anything you *won't* do?"

He paused for a moment. His blue eyes clouded, then hardened with resolve. "Let you go."

"Give me a break." He was sleeping with her for the report. Nothing more.

"I thought you were an engaged woman. I thought I didn't have a chance. I thought you were marrying Brandon for his money."

"Gee. Thanks. What a stellar opinion you must have had of your illicit lover."

"Don't."

"Don't what?"

"If I could go back, and change it all, don't you think I'd do it in a second?"

"I have no idea what you'd do. I don't know you."

"Yes, you do." He took a deep breath, moved forward, and lowered his voice. "Do you remember that first night? In Henry's office?"

Despite herself, the memory bloomed in Jenna's mind. She slowly nodded.

"I wanted you so bad. And I know you wanted me, so don't bother denying it."

Jenna wasn't going to deny it. She wasn't the liar. He was. Besides, she never felt that way before in her life. She'd wanted him all right.

"It was all I could do to stop," said Tyler. "But I did stop. Truth is, I put most of my ethics on hold just to kiss you in the first place."

"You have no ethics," she whispered hoarsely. She didn't want to remember anything good about this man. And that first kiss had definitely ranked as good.

"I have ethics," he said. "But I've discovered that I'll compromise any of them for a chance to be with you." He moved even closer, and Jenna didn't back away. Some wayward part of her still craved his nearness.

What did he mean? Was it good or bad?

Bad. She told herself. Compromising ethics was definitely bad.

"You started out as the subject of an investigation," he continued. "But you ended up as my life."

"Tyler, don't." She reached forward to shut him up. She had to stop the swelling in her chest. She had to stop her body's reaction to his sight and scent and sound. He was a P.I., a spy, a con man, and she couldn't let his practiced words sway her.

He grasped her hand and held it to his chest. "Since that first kiss, I've been looking for a way to make it work. I had my priorities screwed up for a long time, but I'm okay now."

"I'm glad." But his priorities had nothing to do with her. She tried to pull her hand away.

"I can't live without you, Jenna."

He chuckled hollowly. "Candice told me to say that first, but I guess I'm not very good at this."

On the contrary, he was excellent at this. Which was what scared Jenna more than anything. With every word, every gesture, every touch, she found herself wanting to believe him.

"You spied on me for money," she pointed out.

"I tore up the report."

"But you wrote it in the first place."

"And, for that, I am most profoundly and terribly sorry. I was wrong. I should have told you who I was from the beginning. As soon as I knew I was attracted to you. As soon as I knew there could be something between us." He closed his eyes for a second, looking suddenly tired.

Jenna fought an urge to smooth her hand over his brow.

"I should never have taken the job," he said. "I should have told Brandon to find somebody else. But I needed the money."

"I thought you were rich."

"What made you think that?"

"You're a Reeves-DuCarter. You own the hotel, the

corporation. Your brother tosses out million dollar contracts. Your father owns half of the city."

"And I was a broke P.I. up until fifteen minutes ago."

"You mean because Brandon paid you?" This hurt way too bad.

"No. *No!* I told you, I tore up the report. And I told Brandon if he ever comes near you again I'll use every cent of the family conglomerate to bring him down."

"You did?"

Tyler had stood up to Brandon for her? He'd threatened Brandon for her? He'd torn up the report?

"I'm closing the agency, Jenna. The business I've sweated blood for all these years. I caved up there. I asked my dad for a job."

"Why?" She could tell by the sound of his voice that the decision was painful.

"I always thought independence from my family was the most important thing in the world to me." He smiled sadly at her, drawing her closer. "I was wrong. I love you, Jenna. Nothing else even comes close."

His words overwhelmed her. "You're closing your business?"

He nodded.

"For me?"

He nodded again. "Reeves-DuCarter will give me

a good income. Security. I can't ask you to share my life with anything less than that."

"Share your life?"

"I love you so much, Jenna. If you'll let me, I promise I will be nothing but open and honest with you for the rest of our lives."

Jenna blinked back her emotions. Should she believe him? Could she believe him?

He wrapped one hand around her rib cage. "I got it wrong the first time," he whispered. "Please give me a second chance."

"You tore up the report?" she asked, inhaling his scent, subconsciously shifting closer to his warmth.

"I tore up the report." He kissed her gently on the forehead. "Well, okay, technically, not yet. But I will. You can help me."

Jenna felt a smile form. "You had to choose between your business and me?"

"And I chose you. Well, okay, technically, not at first. But I came to my senses. In time. At least I hope it was in time."

Jenna giggled. She couldn't help it. "And here I always thought you were a suave, smooth talker."

"Am I blowing it?"

"No." She shook her head. "You're not blowing it. You're being honest."

Tyler sighed. "Thank goodness."

"I love you, Tyler," she whispered, burying her face against his shoulder.

"Oh, Jenna." He inhaled deeply, cupping her chin, pressing his lips gently against hers.

She lifted her hands to cradle his face, opening her mouth, inviting him into her life.

He kissed her over and over again. Long kisses. Short kisses. Her lips, her cheeks, her eyes, her forehead, oblivious to the few passersby in the lobby.

"I can't live without you," he said.

"Neither can I," she confessed, her heart filling with joy and wonder.

_____Epilogue_____

STRAINS OF A Strauss waltz rose from the string orchestra in the Quayside Hotel ballroom as Tyler gathered Jenna into his arms on the empty dance floor. The full skirt of her wedding dress rustled around his legs. With his palm flat against the small of her back, he guided her gently into their formal first waltz.

"We've never danced together before," she whispered in his ear while their bodies found the rhythm.

"You know what they say." He squinted against the brightening spotlight. The downside of having such a large family, with such a big circle of acquaintances, was the formality of the wedding.

"What do they say?" she asked.

He tightened his hold. Truth was, he couldn't care less what kind of a wedding they had, as long as he got Jenna at the end of it. "They say, if you're good at making love together, you'll also be good at dancing together."

"I think it's the other way around." There was a laugh in her voice. She must have also been smiling, because there were immediate murmurs and oohs from the formally dressed onlookers.

"You sure?" he asked. "Because I think we're pretty good at making love. Why, just the other night—"

"Tyler."

"I distinctly remember—"

"Not now."

"Am I turning you on?"

"You're embarrassing me. There are three hundred people watching us."

"Nobody can tell what I'm saying."

"Still..."

"Like, if I was to tell you your breasts were beautiful."

He heard her swift intake of breath.

"Nobody would know. I could be whispering anything in your ear—"

"I'd know," she said.

"And that's the beauty of it. It's just between you and me. Your turn. Tell me about your underwear."

"No way."

"What color is it?"

"White of course."

"Virginal white. Now there's a fantasy."

Out of the corner of his eye, Tyler saw his and Jenna's parents swing onto the dance floor.

He drew back a few inches to look down at her. "Add one more fantasy to all the amazing nights and days we've had together over the past month?"

Derek and Candice, the best man and the maid of

honor, waltzed by. Candice was frowning and Derek's jaw was tight.

"How did those two do at the job site last week?" Tyler asked. The restaurant renovation was well under way, with the spa phase slated to start in mid-July. The lobby work would be done during the slow fall season.

"Candice and Derek? They're getting worse," she said.

More and more couples swirled out onto the floor. The spotlight went out, giving Tyler and Jenna a welcome bit of anonymity.

"Really?" After some of the stories Jenna had told him, worse was almost inconceivable.

"I swear, they're acting like two-year-olds who need a time-out."

"A time-out?"

"You know. Lock them up together and tell them to work it out before they come back to play with the other children. They nearly came to blows yesterday over whether the wainscoting should have a natural or honey gloss stain."

"Derek argued over the stain color?"

"Can you say micro-manage?"

Tyler chuckled. "I'll see if I can distract him."

"Thank you. I'd appreciate that."

Jenna's father appeared. "May I?" he asked Tyler, smiling down at his daughter.

"Of course." Tyler gallantly stepped away. He'd

only met David and Lorraine McBride yesterday when they'd arrived in time for the rehearsal dinner. But he liked them already.

Lorraine was a practical, no-nonsense, salt of the earth mother. And David had a wonderful sense of humor.

Tyler faded to the side of the dance floor, coming across his father near the head table.

"I've got something for you," said Jackson, reaching into his breast pocket.

"Oh, Dad, no," said Tyler, fearing an exorbitant check.

"It's not money," said his father. "Here." He handed him a white business card.

Tyler squinted in the dim light.

"I've got your job description all worked out," said Jackson.

Tyler Reeves-DuCarter, the card read. *Vice President, Corporate Security*.

"Security?" Tyler looked up in confusion.

"What? You thought I'd give you some cushy junior executive job?" His father chuckled.

"I thought..." He'd thought he was going to be stuck on the thirtieth floor staring at financial reports all day long. But, security. Well, hell, security was something he could really sink his teeth into.

"Funny thing about you," said Jackson. He reached across the table behind him, retrieving his glass of champagne. "You always had it in your head that I wanted to do you boys a big favor by giving you jobs with the company."

True enough. A job with the family company was a get-to-the-top-free card for Derek, Striker and Tyler. Part of the reason Tyler had rebelled was his burning desire to make it on his own.

"Truth is, I need you boys a whole lot more than you need me."

Tyler found that hard to believe. "How so?"

"Take Derek." Jackson motioned to his oldest son where Derek was heading into the express elevator with Candice. They were obviously still arguing.

"Derek could be a CEO with any one of a hundred multinational firms," said Jackson. "He's a whiz with numbers, can spot a solid deal and a non-starter from about five miles.

"And Striker. You don't think Striker could work for any airline he pleased?"

"Well... I guess..." Tyler had honestly never thought about it that way. His brothers were certainly each capable in their own right. But he'd always imagined the company taking care of them, not the other way around.

The lights on the elevators flashed all the way to the top floor where the Lighthouse Restaurant was closed for renovations. Derek and Candice were probably heading up to fight about the wainscoting again.

"I need you on my security force, Tyler," said Jackson. "Barney's been holding off retirement for a few years now. I kept telling him you'd come around."

Tyler turned to stare at his father. "You've been waiting for me?"

"Damn patiently if I do say so myself. For a while there... Well, lets just say your mother worked hard to convince me to wait."

"You think you *need* me." This was a switch.

"No, Tyler. I know I need you. Barney will fill you in next week, but we've got a mole in the electronics division."

"A spy?" It was hard to imagine something quite that cloak-and-dagger at Reeves-DuCarter.

"I know you don't read your annual reports very closely."

Tyler winced. He didn't think he'd even opened the envelope at the end of the last fiscal year. "Not really," he allowed.

"The profits at stake are staggering. Derek cornered Hammond during the wedding photos, and we'll work a deal on this contract somehow But, long term, I need to know who sold me out."

"Right." Tyler nodded. He'd find the spy.

The elevator numbers slid back down to the ballroom level.

Jackson clapped him on the shoulder. "Good to have you aboard, son."

"Thanks, Dad."

The elevator doors slid open, revealing an empty car. Derek and Candice were still in the Lighthouse.

Tyler's attention switched to Jenna. She was dancing with one of her brothers, laughing happily, looking every inch the radiant bride.

His radiant bride. He couldn't wait to carry her over the threshold of his new house on the lakefront. They'd decided to honeymoon right there, and he couldn't wait to start their new life together.

"There you are," said Jenna, slipping her arm into the crook of his elbow. "Your mom wants me to throw the bouquet."

"An excellent idea," said Tyler. He wrapped an arm around her waist and pulled her close, burying his face against her neck. "The sooner we get the formalities over with, the sooner we can get to the wedding night. Did I tell you about the mirror on the ceiling of our new bedroom?"

"Stop." But she was laughing as she protested.

"And I've installed a security camera."

"Where?"

"That'll be a surprise for you later."

"Over here." Tyler's mother motioned to Jenna. "All the young ladies are ready."

"And I have a surprise for you," Jenna whispered in his ear.

"What?"

"My white underwear..."

"Yeah? Lace? Skimpy? High cut?"

"Doesn't exist."

"Oh, man you're getting better at this. When's the last time I told you I loved you?"

"About twenty minutes."

"I'm overdue." He kissed her soundly on the mouth.

The crowd of women waiting on the bouquet toss let out a delighted cheer.

"I love you so much, Jenna," he murmured against her warm lips.

She pulled back a couple of inches, her warm hand going to his cheek, gold-and-green eyes glowing in the soft light. "I can't tell where you end and I begin," she whispered.

"We don't," he said, bending forward for one more kiss. "We never will."

* * * * *

COMING NEXT MONTH...
Don't miss
A GROOM IN HER STOCKING,
author Barbara Dunlop's
latest romantic comedy from Duets!
Volume 90—December 2002
Happy Holidays!

HARLEQUIN®
Duets™

C'mon back to Paxton, Texas!

The Hometown Heartthrobs have returned to delight their fans with a second double Duets volume from author Liz Jarrett!

Chase and Nathan got their stories in Duets #71 in March 2002...

Now it's brother-and-sister time, as Trent and Leigh finally find their own matches and true love not far behind, amidst the all-around wackiness of their neighbors and small-town life!

Look for this exciting volume, Duets #87, in November 2002, as we find out who's...
Meant for Trent and that
Leigh's for Me.

Yahoo x 2!

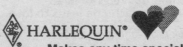
HINTLTW